The Engagement

CHLOE HOOPER

The Engagement

Jonathan Cape
London

Published by Jonathan Cape 2013

2 4 6 8 10 9 7 5 3 1

First published in Australia by Penguin Group in 2012

First published in Great Britain in 2013 by
Jonathan Cape
Random House, 20 Vauxhall Bridge Road,
London SW1V 2SA

www.vintage-books.co.uk

Addresses for companies within The Random House Group Limited can be found at:
www.randomhouse.co.uk/offices.htm

The Random House Group Limited Reg. No. 954009

A CIP catalogue record for this book is available from the British Library

ISBN 9780224096348

The Random House Group Limited supports The Forest
Stewardship Council (FSC®), the leading international forest certification
organisation. Our books carrying the FSC label are printed on FSC®
certified paper. FSC is the only forest certification scheme endorsed by
the leading environmental organisations, including Greenpeace.
Our paper procurement policy can be found at:
www.randomhouse.co.uk/environment

FSC
www.fsc.org

MIX
Paper from
responsible sources
FSC® C016897

For P

PART ONE

I

It started with a letter he wrote, sent that April care of my uncle's estate agency. A thick ivory envelope with my name in elegant type. There was always something too formal about his advances, as though this man's intentions were disguised even from himself. He enjoyed the civilities, but they made me uneasy. Wasn't the etiquette a suit of armour to keep him safe while calling me to battle? I read it standing by the shredder.

> Dear Liese (or whoever you are),
>
> Before you leave Australia to pursue your travels, I wonder if it might not round your experience to see life outside the city? Every visitor should take in the Bush. Warrowill, my sheep and cattle property in western Victoria (itself the third-largest volcanic plain in the world), is close to much pristine bushland, and any amount of wildlife.
>
> I propose you join me on the long weekend of

June 11th–14th, and calculate for three days of your time payment would be $xxxx.

Upon your meeting me on the Friday afternoon, half this fee will be given to you in cash, the other half transferred to your bank account on Monday afternoon at the end of your stay.

Kindly consider this proposal and let me know at your earliest convenience if terms are agreeable.

Sincerely,

Alexander Colquhoun

It was a ridiculous amount he offered, enough to delay my departure for two months, and so it was a relief when, at the appointed time, Alexander, dressed in a blazer and business shirt still creased from the shop, finally picked me up around the corner from the office. He stepped from his oldish Mercedes without meeting my eye. Taking my small suitcase he opened the passenger door, closing it behind me with a deferential nod. He was nervous. I was brusque, lest this whole weekend slide immediately into farce. The dashboard clock read 3.04.

He handed me an envelope. 'Do you want to count it?'

Inside would be cash in those bright colours like play dollars. 'No, I'm sure it's all in order.'

'Perhaps you can now tell by weight?'

'Yes.' Turning, smiling, it was the usual surprise to see his face. He had the kind of looks I regarded as typically Australian: untroubled, slightly sunburnt, slightly elsewhere. If you looked at each feature individually, as sometimes I had for long stretches, they had their complications – an oversize nose; fleshy, inanimate lips, and one blue eye a fraction smaller than the other – but the combination was attractive, probably more so than he realised. He was forty-five, I guessed, his sandy curls now turning grey. I struggled to believe someone this tall and thin could be so preoccupied by flesh. My body, strapped into the car seat's beige leather, matched his sharp angles with hips and breasts. It didn't hide its interests.

'Thank you again for coming.'

'Not at all.'

'I hope you'll enjoy yourself, that this, this won't seem all work to you.'

'That's very thoughtful.'

'I've planned a few things.'

I waited. 'Things for us to do?'

'Yes.' He cleared his throat. 'Things I think you'll like.'

We travelled along the freeway through industrial parks and long, weed-ravaged patches towards the setting sun, and all the time Alexander clasped the wheel with both hands. I could hear him breathing carefully, reminding himself to exhale. He was close enough for me to smell the cedar-scented soap he used, and I knew how his skin would taste, and where that taste changed from the great outdoors to something gamey.

How often does desire arise to cover having nothing to say? Just under my skin I felt that old insinuating heat. Being clothed now seemed more awkward, as if drawing attention to the times we had not been. These three hours in the car would be the most we'd ever spent together, and neither of us was used to talking, to making regular conversation at least. We'd had perhaps twenty meetings and in the beginning most of them were held in near silence. Long sessions with just a request, or – if he was in another kind of mood – a command. When we became better acquainted there were episodes of make-believe, but that was just sex talk. Afterwards, as we reassembled ourselves, I did not ask too many questions, and when he did they were banalities I took for deflection. We were both contriving to forget the fleeting things we'd just seen in the other. This man was shy and I sensed a code of conduct written in the air around him, which I tried to decipher and obey.

Through the car window came country towns – a church, a pub, a war memorial. Then strangely angled farmland. Paddock fences leaned askew; sheep clung to slanted grass (like everything was unstable and tilting). This was a pockmarked version of the country I knew: the Broads, the fens, all the sodden monochrome ground of Norfolk. And soon it was just as flat. A giant bulldozer or lava flow could have passed through once, long ago, and removed any rise or dip. The sky had taken over, stunting the hills and leaving no space for anything else. In the last hour we barely saw another car.

'Is this what you call the bush?' It was more subtle than I'd hoped.

'Patience,' he replied.

I shut my eyes.

The decision to leave Australia had been sudden and, in my head at least, part of me was already gone. I'd bought a new, larger suitcase, shipped home the bulkiest things I'd accumulated, and begun buying little presents for my colleagues in the office. With some of the cash in the envelope I'd purchase an airline ticket. I planned to go via Shanghai, and as we drove I was doing sums on how long I could afford to stay there.

Alexander hummed, a tense mechanical sound, without seeming to realise. Out the window the sky and land were the same tawny colour, the road still a narrow single strip. In the middle of this void stood a Neighbourhood Watch sign, a kind of joke. No houses were in sight, except for those that had been abandoned.

Once I noticed one, more became apparent, and every few minutes I caught sight of a wavering weatherboard cottage moments from falling down, or a careful border of trees surrounding a pile of rubble like rails around a grave.

'What happened to these places?'

'Oh.' Alexander sounded surprised I'd asked. 'The old stone ones were possibly shepherds' huts; the others belonged to soldier settlers. The great sheep stations were broken up for returned servicemen after the First World War. Someone had a starry-eyed dream of creating a yeoman class . . .' His voice trailed off.

Fifty-year-old ruins were sadder than ancient ones. I felt a pang seeing fruit trees someone had planted, but Alexander viewed them as inconvenient. 'My family had to cede land, thousands of acres. Waves of smaller farmers have come and gone, they didn't have a chance, but we've stayed.'

'How long have your family been here?'

'A hundred and sixty years. I suppose that's not long where you're from.'

'It's long enough. Not that this doesn't seem a lovely spot.'

We'd just driven over a rise and seen the mountains. It was as though a backdrop had fallen, perhaps the wrong one. Crags rose up out of the flat grassland, deep purple against the dimming sky. The sun's angle hid any detail on the rock, and the jagged peaks brought to mind a graph of economic doom.

'Behold, the Grampians!' announced Alexander.

'I thought they were in Scotland – did someone move them?'

A tight smile. 'The native name is Gariwerd.'

'Are they the volcanos?'

'Some are.'

'When did they last erupt?'

'Four thousand years ago. The other mountains are sandstone that's faulted and shifted.'

I expected him to say more, to play the tour guide, but he must have been tired from driving. Shadows were settling on the road and his face had changed in the light, although his features did not soften. Staring straight ahead, he gripped the steering wheel with hands that were muscular from farm work, each finger knocked about, the skin around the nails raw pink from being scrubbed so vigorously, while his shirt cuffs were white and starched.

'Three hundred million years ago this was inland sea,' he said, squinting as though to picture it. 'So there were layers of sand and mud and silt, and later earth movements made them lift up and fold over.' Releasing one hand at last, he arched it, wave-like.

I put my hand down on his thigh.

Slowly he smiled again, and I suddenly realised I was actually enjoying myself. I was enjoying myself because soon I'd be leaving and this excursion, amidst the ancient rock, was already lit sentimentally. And so when flocks of bright pink birds flew up from the side of the road, they seemed fantastically exotic; and when a kangaroo the very colour of the darkening paddocks appeared seemingly from nowhere on the bitumen and leapt effortlessly over a fence, some part of me felt light too.

'Did you see that?' My hand didn't move.

'Of course.'

'A kangaroo, wonderful.'

'A wonderful pest. But I'm glad you liked it.'

There was a sign for the Grampians National Park, which was a few kilometres on, although we turned off down a corrugated dirt road, red gravel hitting the sides of the car. This land had been cleared for grazing. I could make out the grey stumps of felled trees, and those that remained looked vigilant. If I glanced away, then back, they seemed to shift on the horizon.

'Who's that up there?' Determined to be a genial guest, I pointed to a bird waiting on a wire.

'A hawk of some kind,' he answered. 'It's the hunting time.'

'He's picked a desolate position.'

'This is my land, actually.'

'Excuse me.'

'I didn't take it personally.'

There came a low bluestone wall, framing a driveway. A wooden sign hung here, marked in faded black cursive *WARROWILL*. We turned and the driveway stretched on, a road unto itself.

'So this is home?' I asked, bewildered.

Ahead of us was a stone building with a pitched roof, machinery strewn around it.

'No, that's the old woolshed.' On the other side of the drive Alexander pointed to a windowless wooden cottage with a series of blank doors. 'And there are the shearers' quarters.'

The driveway became an avenue of poplars, their thick trunks sending up hundreds of leafless sticks. White cockatoos clung to these branches and the air was filled with their dinning: a killing sound like nothing I'd heard before.

Alexander was driving slowly, reverentially. We turned a corner – there was a spread of lawn and then the house rose up from the bare treetops. The second storey came into view: eight upstairs windows and each chimney intricate as a small mausoleum. As the car pulled onto a landscaped circle of gravel, there was the rest of the house. The physical fact of it struck me first: a grand Victorian mansion seemingly carved out of grey-black volcanic rock. The logistics of its construction seemed as complicated as that of a temple in a jungle. Erected in homage to the Old Country, to replicate a stately home, the house had all the period refinements one would expect – a columned vestibule, finials on the roof, classical moulding around the windows – but it was also swathed in a cast-iron veranda to shelter the ground floor from summer heat. I wondered how much the whole place, land included, would be worth.

My instinct was to laugh: a juvenile reflex that often comes upon me when I am in trouble. Mansions require a special quality of awe. But I wanted to laugh at how jarring it was to find this one in the midst of all that was weather-blasted and dirty and hard, and yet I suspected my host would take this as a sign I was delighted by the grandeur, by his choosing this moment to unveil himself as a prince.

'Well, we're here.' Alexander stared at the building with undisguised pride. 'Welcome.'

'Thank you.'

'I hope you'll enjoy your stay.'

It was a cue to say something expansive about his house. Despite being paid to indulge him, though, I felt myself growing stingy with praise, and I climbed out of the car as if I were merely here to give a property valuation.

We were under a big sky, stars emerging. The garden beds and gravel were already covered in dew.

He took my case and led me to the vestibule.

The house had been built precisely so one would feel at its mercy. Following him up the stone steps, I told myself, Do not react. The front door was double regular size and trimmed in stained glass patterned with birds. To the right of the door's eaves was a swallow's nest; a ribbon of shit trailed down the grey wall. But next to it, in the glass, the jewelled birds perched on emerald boughs, garnet berries in their beaks, thinking, Maybe we won't fly north after all.

Opening the door, ushering me into the refrigerated air, Alexander reached for a light switch.

My eyes adjusted and we were standing in a tiled entrance hall with an absurdly high ceiling, and elaborate plaster, paint and wallpaper – the full Victorian works. *Do not react*. Straight ahead of us was a staircase. The stairs began broad enough for a procession and at the landing split off dramatically and became thinner, steeper, curving up on either side to the next floor. Above the landing was an enormous arched window the height of the second floor and outlined in blue glass.

We looked at each other; if I'd wanted to, I might have set him at ease.

'Once I turn the heaters on this will warm up.' There was the slightest tremble now as Alexander spoke. He cleared his throat and looked around, checking all was in order. 'Right.' His gaze settled back on me. 'Let me show you to your room.' Picking up my case, he waited. 'After you, Liese.'

The house's first floor was not so finely decorated. One long corridor, closed doors on either side, it had the look of an institution, a sanatorium perhaps, with bare walls and old carpet. He walked down to one end and pushed open a door to a pink room with a rosebud-quilted single bed and a suite of white furniture. I gave him a sly smile.

'Well,' he glanced at the bed, 'I hope you'll be comfortable here.'

At this familiar moment I expected him to move towards me, to start to touch me. But he stayed where he was.

'Is there anything you need?' he asked.

What was not happening between us had a presence of its own.

'I shouldn't think so.'

'An electric blanket's on the bed.'

I stared at him. 'Thank you.'

'Turn it right up to three,' he said, hands on his hips, businesslike. 'The bathroom's across the hall if you want to freshen up.'

When he left, I stood for a moment staring at the closed door.

There was nothing coded about the message of the room. All the white furniture was slightly undersize: the wardrobe built to accommodate a child's party dresses, the chest of drawers, and the dressing table with matching fine-legged chair designed as if for a sprite. That queasy feeling children get in other people's houses washed over me: time suddenly bending and flexing, to fill fragile hearts with the uncertainty of how it will pass.

I took the cash out of the envelope and stared at it. This was the most money I'd ever had in my hand. Counting it would show the gods how it held my interest, and so instead I started unpacking the clothes I'd brought for this weekend into the too small drawers, hiding the envelope safely underneath.

Cold in the roots of my hair, I walked across the hallway. The bathroom was almost arrogantly unrenovated. My eye went to a heavily stained toilet bowl, and then the antique chain operating the thing. All of it was grimy, although there were signs that after long neglect someone had recently made an effort to clean. On a rusted rail hung two new white towels; little bottles of shampoo, conditioner, body lotion were lined up hotel-like by the sink. These gestures made the rest seem worse.

Leaning against the vanity, my head spinning, I tried to breathe deeply. One of the washbasin's taps had a red enamel disc, the other a disc that read COLD. Icy water spurted from both. Splashing my face, I raised my eyes and caught myself shiver in the small mirror. Feeling like an intruder, I did not look quite right. I did not look worth the money.

II

Four months earlier my uncle had asked me to show a buyer around some properties. 'Gentleman's wanting a *pied-à-terre*,' he said with appropriate scorn, handing over a large envelope of door keys each of which was tagged with an address. I printed out a map. The buyer, Alexander Colquhoun, came to the office and we walked together to the office car.

Blandly handsome, he was also lanky, awkward; if he'd had a hat he would have held it in front of his groin fiddling with its edges like a farmer from an old movie. In the car he sat very straight, as though only unlocked at the knees and hips. I wondered if he hadn't been dressed against his will in Sunday best: the stiff new city clothes and freshly cut hair gave him a dorky, jug-eared look – but handsome, he was definitely handsome.

'You're English,' he said, like it gave us some bond.

'Yes.'

'London?'

'Most recently.'

'And how do you like Australia?'

'Oh, I love it.' Staring straight ahead, I drove through the fog of heat, sensing he guessed I barely knew where I was going.

Not that it mattered. The whole point of this country was that nothing particularly mattered. Compared to London the streets of Melbourne seemed almost casually occupied. There was a lack of critical mass. There was a lack of critical anything. People felt obliged to tell me that *The Economist* had ranked this 'the world's most liveable city'. Miles from anywhere else, the population believed their town to be enchanted – and I wished someone would wave the wand over me.

I had come to start a new life: for the past six weeks I'd trailed my uncle, learning his ways. To succeed in this job, he advised, one needed to be hard-working, honest, a good communicator and, most importantly, attractive. That was the main prerequisite, and so I began dressing in a close-fitting grey suit and fawn heels, the plastic nametag *Liese Campbell* pinned to the breast of my white shirt. My uncle had assigned me to his rental division. Driving a newly leased VW Polo full of property brochures, I'd arrive at some stranger's house to unfurl and plant my flag in his front garden bed: OPEN FOR INSPECTION. Then, in the orange glow of afternoon, I held a clipboard while in trooped couples, divorcees, students, down-on-their-lucks, all of them thinking, Choose me, write my name on your form. Here, 'real estate', as they called it, was a type of public theatre – all the community felt entitled to look through their neighbours' houses. Meanwhile I inhaled the rising damp and reeled off platitudes about these caves.

That was basic training. After a few weeks my uncle moved me to the higher-end properties; he thought my accent would lend some class to the proceedings, a colonial thing. This was a course in improvisation, and the people I met, conceivably also taking the course, were acting the need for shelter. I was acting that I wasn't out of control. Lifting Ovid from the shelf of a 'deceased estate', I'd started reading *Metamorphoses* like a self-help book. Somewhere within its pages would be a story of a 35-year-old woman who could change at will into a bird or a fawn or a real-estate agent. Why not? There was something about being in other people's houses, a frisson of freedom: perverse, I suppose. Released from my normal life, I stood in rental properties monologuing on courtyards, laundry facilities, parking spaces – quoting prices I could not afford as if these figures were a test of one's true inner worth.

Tenants – especially men – listened to the spiel and took me seriously. If a man and I were alone, I tried to show him any bedroom quickly, but even so, often something basic – a shared apprehension of illicit possibilities – passed between us. He would look at me and sign a contract, then a cheque, and I knew he wished he were paying for something else.

At the first places I presented to Alexander Colquhoun, he was in a hurry to leave, as though we were trespassing, and gazing into other people's built-in wardrobes, even empty ones, was shameful.

We were in a district where, as far as I could tell, a whole cul-de-sac of apartment buildings had just the week before sprung out of the dust of reclaimed industrial land. My uncle, who had bought a number of one-bedroom units off the plan, now needed to sell them, and I wanted to broaden my repertoire; it would be thrilling to make a sale. Each apartment had been decorated neutrally, stylishly, so buyers might step into their very own fantasy. Everything in the manner of a four-star hotel – sparkling surfaces, bedspreads pulled taut, handtowels no one had touched fanned under expensive soaps – but in each was a photo frame with the same generic image of a bride re-virgined, posing amidst flounces of white in a horsedrawn carriage.

These were the kind of places which in my old life I'd drafted. Back in England I'd trained as an interior architect, hoping to create airy, modernist dream-houses. Instead I spent years designing boom apartments with sleek surfaces to be erected quickly and cheaply. At home this work had slowed right down, but here there had been no bust. As my uncle put it, the locals just pumped minerals over to China then stacked higher and higher 1BR or 2BR boxes for spivs making a killing in resource stocks who needed to diversify their portfolios.

We saw three apartments on that first morning, none of which were to Mr Colquhoun's liking. Nevertheless I smiled and I continued smiling as we visited new addresses in the afternoon where, with an almost regal air of bemusement, he coughed into his fist and conveyed that such characterless places were beneath him.

Standing by the floor-to-ceiling windows of a 27th-floor apartment, he looked out at a shrunken Melbourne, with toy skyscrapers and toy trains running by little patches of garden no one had watered, and said, 'Modern cities are all the same.'

'I think old ones are.'

'Is there a building out there that's in any way original?'

Sighing, I thought, He's probably right, what am I doing here?

This was a place to while away a life, not to find oneself – if that wasn't too dated an ambition. Self-discovery was meant to happen in the Third World, surrounded by others' squalor. A surge of dissatisfaction came over me, at not being somewhere more exotic, more testing. Even these buildings seemed content to not be very interesting.

'No comment?' He seemed eager for conversation yet his mode was to play the curmudgeon.

A wall of plate glass was an inch in front of me, then the sheer drop. I felt vertigo and some other tension: my shoulder happened to be touching the side of his bicep. 'It's not a fair sample. Plenty of contemporary buildings are as exciting as any gothic cathedral.'

He smiled as though moved by my naïveté.

As I stepped from the window, my reflection shimmered – I straightened my shirt, pulling it smooth over my bust, aware Alexander was watching. I was more curvaceous than suited my personality; carrying around all this pale flesh seemed indiscreet, like I'd made some lewd genetic choice. Each morning, to counteract it, I pulled my hair into a tight blond ponytail and wore very little makeup, hoping to be fetchingly wan without looking tubercular; an exotic in a place where everyone else was tanned.

I brushed at a stray hair and turned towards the apartment's kitchen area. 'So what do you think?'

'I'm not sure that's actually for cooking.'

'Have you seen the restaurants around here?' I stayed close to him. 'You won't want to cook. And this newness,' I said the word in parody of fogeyism, 'which you find off-putting is really part of the convenience.' Touching his arm, pointing out the Miele appliances: 'No one's come in and broken everything.'

'You don't think the ceilings seem very low?'

'It's just that you're so tall.'

Alexander walked around the rooms again. It was as cramped as he said, and I couldn't not notice the build of him through his clothes. He didn't move the way I thought a farmer ought. He was lean and muscular, but had a high level of physical unease. Something about his body – I presumed his gangliness – embarrassed him, and he opened doors for me bowing slightly, in a style suggesting both deference and satire. The more he disguised his nature, the more aware of it I was. He even smelled slightly different. Was it the scent of the farm? All his politesse drew attention to what was raw.

As the afternoon wore on, he seemed to imply we were looking for a place to suit us both, that I'd passed a test and turned from his *bête noire* into a co-conspirator. Did I enjoy this assumed intimacy? Yes. I was trying to sell him a property and, I guess, in a new city where I knew next to no one, even these appointments counted as company.

'Now, this would be nice,' I said, peering into a bathroom.

It had a freestanding, double-ended bath, a wall-mounted basin, limestone tiles.

'You're sure you like it?' He whispered although we were alone.

'Very much.'

'And the colour?'

'It's subtle, restful.'

Alexander was beginning not to want to disappoint me. 'Well,' he shrugged, looking sheepish, 'I wouldn't have thought of buying something like this, but perhaps it isn't a bad idea.'

'Shall we move on?' It was best to stay upbeat.

'Where are you taking me now?'

'I think this last place will really appeal to you.' I smiled optimistically. 'I can see you in it.'

'You can see me in it.' He met my gaze. 'And what am I doing?'

'You are living your lifestyle dream, as the brochure promises.'

Alexander laughed without making a sound, and followed me back down in the tight lift to the close little car.

When we arrived at this last apartment of his tour, my hand fumbled in the envelope, trying to divine the right key. He glanced at me expectantly. If I picked the key without checking the tag and it opened this door, we would cross the threshold straight into our new life.

The key did not fit.

I looked now at the labelled tags and pulled out the correct one. I turned it in the lock, and I stood in the doorway, feeling a shiver of déjà vu. I could predict the apartment's exact layout: it was just like those I'd been drafting before I was retrenched. An almost identical plan had been on my computer on the last day of work, when the boss brought in a cake – as though this were merely a birthday – and I ate a slice, then loaded a box with my belongings, before I and three others were shown to the door. It was the Global Financial Crisis; everyone was losing their job. My colleagues had all handled their cake nervously. These days English firms were contracting designers in Vietnam or India, and I'd breezily told my boss I'd long been planning to go and work in Australia anyway. 'You see, I have an uncle in property . . .'

Now I didn't touch Alexander's arm, I didn't dare as I led him through the living-dining area to the master bedroom, with its bed crowned by a little pink-velvet, heart-shaped cushion (some developer's idea of a personal detail), to the dressing room, a narrow mirrored area, in which I could hear his breathing change. He paused to take in the bathroom with its shower big enough for two, and broad marble countertops. Everything was too suggestive – the right size or shape for other things.

Quickly I steered us back to the kitchen.

'The oven's a good make,' Alexander admitted. 'It wouldn't do badly at all.'

I thought of those dreams where one finds an extra room in a small house. He seemed to see extra rooms – spaces invisible to me – one after the other, and I realised he was actually moving towards the purchase.

'Yes,' he nodded, picturing himself here, 'perhaps this is —'

'You know,' I interrupted, 'I can understand why these places don't appeal.'

'No, I'm thinking perhaps it could work.' He looked over at me, expecting I'd be pleased.

'But you don't really like it.'

Alexander straightened, confused. His brow creasing, he glanced around as though he'd just lost something.

'You'd never be happy here,' I went on, moving us back to the bedroom. 'I feel sure of it.'

'Wrong lifestyle dream?' He sounded annoyed, but he was following.

I can only think the apartment was too familiar. That seeing all its uncanny resemblances to the places I'd designed in London, along with the sharper humiliation of my recent firing, made me want to somehow tarnish it. The fittings were new and smooth and begging to be soiled – that was the whole point of this kind of design. And that was why I led sober Mr Colquhoun to the double bed and began unzipping my skirt, then rolling down my tights. And that's why I lay on the mattress and lowered myself onto the little pink-velvet pillow, positioning it just underneath my arse.

How innocent or experienced was he? I could feel his hipbones when he lay on top. And when I was on him, his large hands, calloused, held my hips as if he were weighing me. How long since he'd touched someone in this way? I could not tell.

Afterwards, while Alexander was dressing, his face flushed, his mannerisms just slightly overstated, he checked the pockets of his moleskin trousers, half removing a roll of cash. Seeing the way I beheld it, he turned from me. He was fumbling with the roll.

'Perhaps I ought to help get the quilt cleaned,' he murmured. 'Please, take a hundred.'

'Only a hundred?'

I realised he didn't know what to do. There must have been something about the way I'd gone about this that made him think he ought to pay for it – and now I did too. Taking the roll, I peeled off two more hundred-dollar notes. 'It's half-price,' I said, 'because I like you.'

Hands trembling, I went about straightening the white bedclothes and my own clothes. Later, deadlocking the door after us, there was only one thing I felt bad about – the little heart pillow now had a mark on it. While he wasn't looking I'd dabbed at the stain with a towel then left it turned over on the bed.

III

I hated houses like this. Shutting the door of the pink bedroom, I retraced my steps along the dim upstairs hallway. Fur-like dust covered everything, every coiled, frilled detail: the carved eaves around each closed door, the banister of the staircase and its railings. At college we barely studied Victorian architecture. It was considered mildly embarrassing, too full of pomp and sagging grandeur, too historical. If anyone referenced the aesthetic it was to be ironic. But walking down the steep stairs, I tried to draft a plan of the layout in my head. The first floor was one long rectangle, bedrooms on either side; the ground floor opened onto the entrance hall with its two grand adjacent rooms, and further along, to each side of the staircase, separate corridors led left and right.

Alexander had switched off the entrance hall's light, and in the dark I placed each step carefully, feeling for the stair, until my foot landed hard on the tiled floor. I could not tell in which direction to now go.

I paused, listening.

Past the left-hand corridor was a faint light. I walked towards it and entered what must have been the old servants' wing. The dimensions were tighter, the ceilings lower. It smelt of earth.

'Hello,' I called.

'This way,' Alexander answered.

I followed his voice into a kitchen, large enough for a fleet of cooks and unchanged since their departure. Scuffed red linoleum on the floor and cream cupboards running to the ceiling, lining each wall. An antique Aga was embedded in their midst – beside it stood Alexander.

'You are here,' he said softly, almost bowing. 'You are actually here.'

Yes, I am, I thought. And I should have known it would be like this, the house matching his faded decorum.

He looked like a teenager who'd shot up without broadening. On his long thin torso his apron was too small. Behind him a frying pan spat but he stood as if overwhelmed, a strange, sweet smile on his face. 'Are you hungry, Liese?'

'I am.'

'And you eat meat?'

'I do.'

'I suppose I should have asked.' His voice was tight as he tried to sound casual. 'It's a scratch meal tonight, but an English specialty – kidneys. Tomorrow I promise to cook properly.' He turned back to the stove. 'Do you mind a slightly pissy taste?'

I hesitated. 'Is there an alternative?'

'A not so pissy taste.'

'Oh.'

I remembered how in the different places we met, properties for sale or rent, he would occasionally look in people's pantries, scan their cookbooks.

After our first liaison, Alexander rang once a week to tell me when he'd be in town. Each time I gave him a different address. He would knock on the door and I would lead him into a 'spacious 3BR entertainer's townhouse, showcasing stylish architectural vision in a dream lifestyle location'. Or a 'refurbished bluestone church featuring infinite breathtaking possibilities'. Or the bay window of a 'freestanding Victorian with tuck-pointed façade and excellent rear access'. (All the copy eventually sounding like singles ads.) That he had to pay me was taken for granted. He would hand me a white envelope with cash inside it. I would spread out a towel on the bed, undressing myself then him.

In the beginning he was serious, worried he might somehow cause offence – even in the most basic moments all that breeding never quite left him – whereas I had to fight the itch of comedy. I considered charging him exorbitantly just to touch me but throwing in fellatio for free, or adding a tax if he gave over the money in a way that struck me as begrudging. Why not be paid for degrees of penetration, with a surcharge for other objects? Or a fee for different surfaces, including penalties for carpet burn?

I owed money, you see. And every morning I woke with this figure imprinted on my eyelids. Debt's gnawing was like a small insect burrowing deeper and deeper towards my brain. Cash was the only analgesic.

So, we would be lying on someone else's bedspread, their photographs and ornaments arranged carefully on the bedside cabinet, the things they wished to keep from view still hidden inside, and I'd be thinking, I can't believe I'm doing this. Using these rooms was the transgression, taking his money just an element of our game. This game involved leaving normal life and returning unscathed. Back in the office, the towel we'd used jutted from my bag; my workmates believed I'd taken up swimming. I assumed Alexander knew he was my sole customer ever. I also assumed he preferred I didn't mention that to be the case. It was a game until it was not. Then we were anyone – everything. Total strangers, trying to forget our own names. It always worked best to imagine we'd never see each other again.

'All right.' Alexander was scanning the kitchen, crossing off an invisible checklist.

On the shelves of the cream cupboards, amongst the crockery, were prize ribbons from various agricultural shows. There was also a promotional calendar, turned to the June pin-up of an award-winning bull.

Lifting the pan off the stove, Alexander found it hard to meet my eye. He started towards the kitchen door. 'Please follow me.'

Back in the hallway, the darkness was intense, almost alive.

After a few steps I brushed a wall.

'I'm sorry, come in this direction,' his voice beckoned.

Finding the strings of his apron, I kept hold of it, moving forward as he did. The cooking had brought out the kidneys' odour. It was fetid, like walking into garbage cans.

'I know my way around with my eyes closed.' He flicked a switch and a chandelier flared on, a hundred sulphur-tinged droplets, illuminating the dining room.

Along one wall, French doors were festooned with bustles of magenta velvet. The other walls held a crammed assembly: a row of mounted fox heads, carved emu eggs on silver stands, antique sporting trophies, and engravings of favourite stallions, their legs splayed like rocking horses. In the centre of the room was a long table that could have seated twenty but was set for two. Three white camellias were in a crystal centrepiece, the arrangement slightly awkward.

Alexander deposited the pan of kidneys on a sideboard, alongside a toaster and loaf of bread. 'Please, sit.'

'Thank you.' My back to him, I listened as he carved two slices of bread, putting them in the toaster's slots.

'Sorry,' he was tapping his fingers on the sideboard, 'it gets too cold if I do it in the kitchen.'

His sensitivity was not without charm. He was taking this seduction seriously, but we'd already bypassed all the normal intimacies and as he stood behind me striking a match, I tried not to shiver. He leaned closer, then over me, his thick fingers trembling as he lit the table's candles. He turned off the chandelier and the room seemed to jerk. From behind me again, he poured wine into my glass.

I felt him watching me drink, checking my reaction. 'It's delicious.'

'I thought you would like it.' The toaster made its electric *ping* and Alexander served up the kidneys on two plates. 'Please, start.'

I raised the fork to my mouth. This meat was soft and firm and dense and *pissy*. 'That's powerful,' I offered.

He untied the apron and sat down opposite. 'The kidneys have been souring in there.'

My eyes were still adjusting. 'In where?'

'In the animal,' he said. 'Some people perfume them with wine and herbs, but I think they should taste of what they are. Why pretend it's something else? The animal is the animal. Past generations respected animals by not wasting anything. The heart, the liver, the lights, the bladder even.' Talking about what he knew – meat – seemed to relax him. I wondered if he was entirely serious or whether this butchery chat was a way of dealing with his shyness. Either way, Alexander could not disguise a hopeful look: the introvert's pleasure at the prospect of being drawn out. 'Usually we eat the outer flesh,' he explained earnestly, 'but this is the inside of the animal and it smells like the inside of the animal. The kidneys don't get any light, any air; they don't get any exercise.'

This was *Pygmalion* done with offal. 'How did you learn to cook?'

'I didn't really have a choice.' He shrugged. 'No one else could.'

Alexander refilled both our glasses. 'People today get their tidy little plastic-wrapped piece of steak at the supermarket, and they don't even know what part of the animal they're eating.'

I was looking at him as if for the first time. He had a nerdish hold on his enthusiasms, and his face was flushed – the zeal had risen to the surface. So this is what interests you, I thought. It was moving, in a way. Until now I'd not had much idea of what he cared about.

A clock panted as if the house itself were drawing breath.

'I've been thinking of inviting you here for a while, Liese.'

'It's very nice to leave the city for a few days.'

'I wanted us to spend some time together.'

I glanced down, so I'd appear the one who was embarrassed.

'Okay.' He clasped his hands together. 'Where are we up to in the story of your life?'

'Well . . .' I smiled, as though touched he cared. He wanted me to fall for him – or to act it out, at least. He was paying to woo me, a routine much more intricate than pretending we'd never met before and would never meet again. My announcement that I was leaving the country had excited Alexander's interest in my past, and I wondered which past would now advance things between us – one full of dirty stories or my actual, very normal Norwich girlhood. Here in the dark I could use either.

'This,' he gestured around the room as if we were sitting in a palace, 'this must all seem very . . . well, I hope it doesn't make you uncomfortable.' His head to one side, his lean neck veered from the business shirt. 'What I'm trying to say is, I don't take all this seriously. I mean, I don't let it define me.'

'No, of course not.'

'Because these places can, if you let them.' He paused, waiting for me to ask the right question, then proceeded regardless. 'The house was built by my great-great-grandfather, son of a Scottish blacksmith.' Nodding towards a portrait over the fireplace. 'He came at sixteen and made himself a wool baron. From nothing. He died with a hundred thousand acres.'

'Is he buried in one of them?'

'Not one that I own any more.' He seemed distracted by the thought.

'And you live here . . . by yourself?'

Alexander smirked. 'I'm not married, if that's what you're asking.'

I laughed like the thought hadn't occurred to me. 'Do you ever find this house too big?'

'Why? Is this another place you wouldn't sell me?'

'To be honest, I have more experience with modern architecture.'

He studied the tabletop. 'I've read some girls can make a lot of money in your field.'

'Property's really more lucrative at the top.'

'You *help out* in your uncle's business.' His intonation suggested real estate was a known front. 'But I meant your other field.'

'Oh.' So not my Norwich girlhood then.

'Some of you put yourselves through university, finishing up with the degree and even investment properties.' Alexander smiled briefly, turning his wineglass in his hand. 'Anyway, what I'm trying to say is that your different jobs show you have a certain amount of get-up-and-go, of ambition, and I don't think that's any bad thing.'

I wondered whether I was meant to take this as a joke.

He looked up at me. 'Have you set a date to leave Australia?'

'Not yet.'

'You've bought the ticket?'

'Soon.' In fact hopefully next week.

'I see. Where are you planning to go?'

Moving the kidneys around on my plate: 'I'd like to travel home through Asia. I've never been —'

Alexander straightened. 'You're not going to try to work there?'

I hesitated because actually I was. A designer friend in Shanghai reported new buildings were going up daily, that it would be easy enough to find a job.

'I only ask because I imagine in your trade there'd be a hell of a lot of competition.'

'Yes, possibly.'

'Not that you wouldn't have advantages.' Perhaps he was trying to stay positive, but his wholesome face looked strained.

'Thank you.'

'Tell me about the brothel you worked in.'

Had I told him a story about one during our meetings?

One Monday morning my uncle's receptionist, Maria, announced to the office that over the weekend she had been to an open day at a local brothel. All the women had instantly stopped work to gather around her cubicle, eager for the details. 'Do they hold these events often in Australia?' I'd asked hopefully. (It wasn't like one could learn how to ply this trade by reading up in the library.) No, the open day was a one-off. The brothel, the largest in the Southern Hemisphere, was being listed on the Australian stock exchange and this was part of the publicity campaign. For a 'gold coin donation' – one or two dollars dropped into a bucket – that would go to a charity aiding sexually abused children, a 'hostess' with a cigarette in one hand and a rum and Coke in the other, who may or may not have been a hooker, led around Maria and a group of fifteen others.

Apparently it was as though all the brothel's staff had been coached to use the words *hygiene* and *safety* as frequently as possible. In the industrial-sized laundry, the visitors were told they could have been in the bowels of a hospital – all linen was washed at highest temperatures with antibacterial disinfectant – by the bright yellow, two-metre-high bin where condoms were relegated, they heard about trained hazardous-waste specialists; by a spa bath, about regular inspections from an environmental health officer; then, taking in a bed custom-made to accommodate four people, they were given assurances of rigorous monthly STD checks. Everyone nodded solemnly, presumably wishing they could just see the people fucking.

'The brothel in which you worked . . . outside London,' Alexander tried to jog my memory.

I didn't say anything.

'Did you have to line up in a row and get picked? I mean I, I imagine you were always picked first.'

'It wasn't that sort of place.'

'I see.' He waited for me to expand. 'It was a nice sort of place?'

'It was a nice brothel, exactly.'

He nodded. 'An exclusive one?'

'Very exclusive.'

'But it was time to move on and so you decided to come to Melbourne and strike out on your own?'

'More or less.' For some reason I couldn't get in the mood. I hadn't drunk enough to make a confession and lie back on his table, hitching up my skirt.

He looked at me as he sometimes did in the apartments, searching for a higher truth. It was always daytime when we met, and some places did not run to blinds or curtains: unless the room had little natural light, we saw each other in too fine detail. This made me want to blindfold him. If he wouldn't close his eyes, I wouldn't either. Really I preferred to face away.

'During your career has there ever been anyone you regretted working with?'

'Hmmm.' I made as if to remember. It didn't take much; he was happy enough doing this routine alone.

'Presumably you'd be very fortunate not to look back with, I don't know, dismay at some clients.' He was nodding, still trying for a story. 'I just wondered if there was anyone you wished you hadn't taken on?'

'Can we talk about something else?'

I hoped he'd take my reticence for part of the performance.

'I'm not trying to embarrass you.' Alexander considered a puzzle within the candle's flame. 'But, yes – so, are you studying yourself?'

'Ah, no.'

'I thought you might be using the extra funds to take a course, fine arts or literature maybe?'

'Why?'

'Well, with the money you make from your profession.'

'Alexander,' I tilted my head flirtatiously, 'are these the sort of questions to ask a girl the first time you bring her home?'

While we'd discussed the rigours of my imaginary profession before, now, out of bed, I did find some hard-wired prudery kicking in. 'I don't think of myself in those terms,' I explained firmly. My keywords were *eros, cash, debt reduction*. 'And I suppose talking about it like this with you feels strange.'

'Does it?'

My fingertips touched my collarbone as I brushed back my hair. 'It makes me shy.'

'I'm sorry, really,' he said, although he didn't seem sorry. He seemed put out, frustrated that I was blocking him, even though it was done in a teasing style.

Alexander met my eye briefly. 'Do you have to give away a large cut of your pay?'

'I don't follow.'

'To a pimp.'

'No,' I said sarcastically. 'I'm an independent contractor.'

'Well.' He arranged his knife and fork side by side on his plate. 'It must give you a lot of freedom. You can move around from place to place. Meet people.' From the neck up, he had reddened, turning as dignified and stiff as the man in the painting. 'Good for you, being your own boss. Who wants to spend their life in an office?'

In my old life, every morning by seven a.m. I was on the tube to the East End. For ten hours a day I stared at a black computer screen, manipulating the red, green, yellow lines of computer-aided design to create walls and floors and windows. The program infected everything I did: if I dropped something on the ground I'd think, Control Z, the shortcut for 'undo'. As I walked down the street, trees before me morphed into 3D lines as if I were drafting the layers of their canopies; buildings rose in the air, rotating, zooming in and out. And when unwelcome visitors entered my thoughts, I drew a box around them and they were deleted.

I reached across the dining table for Alexander's hand but he did not move.

'You have to be very brave to be in your line of work,' he said with po-faced generosity.

'I suppose so.' Upstairs I'd discovered my mobile phone had no reception. I'd told my uncle – the first person who'd notice I was missing – that I was going on a hiking trip with an old schoolfriend.

Alexander seemed to read my mind. 'Presumably someone always knows where you're working.'

My expression must have shown no one did.

He stood, regarding my knife and fork, arranged differently to his. As the meat had cooled its odour was of bodies. 'I'm sorry this meal wasn't more of a hit. I promise not to cook it for you again.'

'It was delicious. I just wasn't that hungry.'

'The dogs will enjoy the leftovers.' He wiped his palms against his trousers before picking up my plate, and smiled, closed-mouthed. 'You might prefer dessert?' He waited a second by the door. 'No. Tea or coffee, perhaps? I'll give you a moment to think about it.'

I stayed seated at the long table.

The candles were burning down; I reached out to stop a dribble of wax falling on the wood.

To become accredited as an interior architect in Australia I had only to do a short course. It would have taken a weekend, and I could have then earned more than I did shepherding around renters and buyers. But I kept finding reasons to put it off. In truth I was sick of the design work I'd been doing. Most of my clients didn't just want shelter, they wanted a temple dedicated to themselves: a kitchen to nourish their spirits, a bathroom to nurture their souls.

Why was selling these places easier than drafting them? Because these building were already built, the colours and materials chosen, their success or failure of no consequence to me. And the money Alexander gave me more than made up the difference in income. Plus I worked shorter hours and had access to locations for us to meet.

Every time we parted I locked another door behind us, and I felt intense relief which soon gave way to exhilaration, but also the groggy realisation that this had to stop. *Although*, an impish voice taunted, *who exactly is getting hurt?* He had a good time. I did too – and each day there were new headlines about the global economy contracting, about multitudes overseas losing their jobs and savings and homes. It was hardly a time to turn down work.

'Live the dream!' – they don't stop telling you that after you've been fired and had your credit cards suspended. And no one says which dream to live: the good or bad one? Seeing Alexander soothed the tedium of the office, gave it charge. All the tagged keys hanging on the back wall became magical, each one able to open onto a new exotic wood. So would I have considered expanding my operation? No.

One detail about the brothel's open day stuck in my head.

The group were standing in a room lit green. The carpet, although new, was already worn down around the bed. A security guard who'd joined the tour had a rat's tail of bleached hair winding down his neck, and wraparound mirrored sunglasses which he raised up and down in a vaudeville-style move to check out the more attractive visitors. He told the group each bed was fitted with a discreetly located panic button in case there was trouble. 'If the girls can get to it, that is,' he added with a smirk.

I stood up from the dining table.

The door was ajar. He had turned on the hall light and I walked through the cold to the drawing room. Facing the doorway was a tall rectangular gilt-edged mirror and all the room – and anyone who entered – was caught in its reflection.

Had I considered being paid before?

Of course I had. Even before I was fired. Each month the bills rolled in, an ever fiercer wave, and despite my daily commute to that computer screen in Hoxton, I was travelling further into debt. Rain streaked the office windows like exclamation marks: *Do something! Act!* But the money owing multiplied. It was like an organism with its own moods, its own weather, over which I had no control. One credit card and then I was offered another credit card, and it seemed a way to wipe the slate clean. I'd rather have fallen into debt for more sympathetic reasons, but in this world you can become insolvent by just trying to look your best. How else to find a mate than by getting poorer still, wearing the right clothes to the right club and ordering the right drink to meet the right person? But why had I been doing this? Did I think a mate could bail me out? Or did I want children? Could I stay with anyone for longer than it took to conceive? Would anyone stay with me? These subterranean questions spooled on and on.

When, after a typically expensive night out, one man arose from my bed and walked down the gnome-size stairs of my studio's mezzanine, I thought, You will leave like you've had some victory, and I still don't know how to pay my phone bill. From any direction it was five paces to the door. The kimono I was wearing suddenly looked gaudy. As he retrieved his clothes off my floor and coins fell out of the pockets, I scooped them up, winking. Was that self-regard or self-loathing?

In Alexander's drawing room there was a general air of permission – whoever had decorated this had given herself licence. The walls were covered in mustard-coloured silk. Money had been deposited in dusty furnishings and transformed into class. I stood surrounded by oriental vases, an ormolu clock on an upright piano with attached brass candelabra, exotic birds arranged in a glass case, their expressions suitably eerie. It was like a provincial museum you'd visit because nothing else was open.

In the centre of the room, amidst the antiques, was a squat couch not dissimilar to the one my parents owned, upholstered in a heavy autumnal print. It seemed someone disapproving of their forebears' high living had chosen the most drab, utilitarian design.

I heard his footsteps.

He loped into the room holding a block of chocolate, and must have caught derision in my expression. 'What is it?'

'Nothing.'

'Tell me.'

'Oh,' I said casually, 'it's just that couch.' In strangers' houses, sometimes we would laugh about their taste.

'What's wrong with it?'

I shook my head. Who was I to judge his furnishings? My

family had nothing of provenance other than an old dictionary and a slightly older silver teapot. Nerves made me sound disdainful: 'It just looks out of place, when everything else is in such fine taste.'

'No one's ever commented on it before.'

'Well, it's certainly comfortable,' I said. Kicking off my heels I displayed myself on it in camp apology, offering him the invitation I presumed he expected – the point of all this. As though I were really alone, I undid the buttons of my blouse, easing up my skirt, moving my fingers underneath. It was so easy to shock him. His repression turned me on, and made him complicit. We were a team.

But now he stayed by the doorway. 'Do you ever think of anything else?'

Here was something new.

I turned to him. 'You *are* paying me to have sex.'

'Really?' Alexander sounded genuinely angry. 'Is that really what you think?'

'To have sex if you want to.'

'I see.' He was trying not to appear wounded. 'That *is* what you think.' His hand went to his forehead. 'Listen, I'm, I'm not good at this sort of thing. Okay? Dating and the whole act you're supposed to put on.' The hand was thrown down again in exhaustion. 'Can't you see? I just want to know who you are, Liese, who you really are.'

Something about the way he said this made me uneasy. 'I want that too,' I answered weakly.

'Do you really?'

'Yes.' My voice was too high.

'Then can we agree to start again?'

I nodded.

'To start from scratch and see who the other is?'

I felt this man's isolation sharply. Surrounded by ancestral clutter, he was living in a time as well as a place that was remote, and this made sense of an impression I'd had before. Under the prickly carapace he seemed naïve, naïve and at too great a disadvantage. The hint of sadism I thought I'd detected during dinner was just the gracelessness of someone unused to spending time with others. He needed to be treated gently: within his own house he wanted his lust to be hidden from view. Yet as I went to Alexander and lay my head against his chest, and as he laid his head on mine, I could not turn the idea of sex off. Almost disconnected from me, my hands crept down and started unbuckling his trousers.

He moved me away.

As he crossed his arms his clothes became too wide for his frame. 'You must be tired. It was a long drive,' he said sadly. 'I think perhaps it's time for bed.'

Picking up my shoes, sighing, I followed him back through the tiled hall, up the wide staircase.

My blouse was half undone, and I could feel the cold on my chest. I had to turn this night around, to fix its failure, but I'd drunk too much wine after all. When we reached the pink bed-room, the walls made me bilious. They were the Crayola colour children use to draw the skin of white people.

'Won't you come in?' I dropped the shoes on the ground.

'Not so loud.'

For a split second I wondered if there *was* a child asleep here.

I finished taking off my blouse and skirt, then my underwear, adding to the pile.

We'd never been together in a kid's room before. Pouting: 'Will you show me what I'm supposed to do?'

Usually I only had to make some minor move – take off my watch even – and Alexander was on a string. I sat on the high single bed and beckoned him towards me. He came closer, and then, almost grudgingly, closer again until he was near enough for me to reach over a second time to undo his fly.

'Do you think we could turn out the light?' He sounded weary.

I looked up and caught the row of pony figurines along the mantelpiece. 'Okay.'

Moving to the switch Alexander glanced back at me – an expression as though he'd just won something.

The room went black and I felt a shiver of anticipation; the darkness was blindfolding. Raising my hand to my face, I could not see it, and I lay waiting for him to brush against me, for his breath on my skin. Laughing: 'Where are you?'

No answer.

He knew the house so well, I thought, he must have remembered by heart where to stand, which floorboards made no noise, but I heard his breathing and I waited. Sometimes, at the start, he didn't say very much, expecting me to take care of conversation. We'd be in a different apartment but physically each episode began in a familiar way. His approach tentative at first, then opening my legs with his knees, lowering himself down; his mouth would find the same places, and then, in the same order, his hands were on my skin, calloused fingers touching me as though he wore rough gloves.

Lying here now, stretched out, ready, I could make out his heartbeat, sense his hands inches from mine. I was determined not to say his name aloud, not to be the one to speak first.

'Alexander.' When finally I broke, my voice was plain although he'd want me to be scared, girlish. 'Alexander, stop it.'

Still I waited – there was the faintest ripple of glass as the wind charged by – and only slowly did I realise: the sound of his watch was in fact my watch, with its cheap mechanism; the sound of his breathing was really my own lazy breath, the heartbeat belonged to my body. This room now seemed to shrink, closing in until it was as small as a room in my head. He had been here, and now he was not. Turning off the lights, Alexander had disappeared, leaving me to lie alone in the pure dark.

IV

That first morning I lay still in the tall single bed, waiting for proof I was awake. The room was narrow, boxlike, with high pressed-metal ceilings. Over the years scouring sunlight had turned the pink walls sallow, this country's light ageing everything. In the bright white sky out the window I watched the green cloud of a cypress pine. The tree's branches were swaying, but only silence, or whatever dream had tagged me in my sleep, now reverberated. I listened harder. It was unnaturally quiet and I wondered if Alexander was still in the house.

I did not want to get up and start this whole routine again, but unfolding slowly into the cold I stood and walked to the window. A formal garden surrounded the house, dominated by a vast lawn. From this vantage I could make out circular patterns where someone had recently mowed. The lawn was framed by a privet hedge, then further, as far as I could see, there was flat, verdant farmland – no other buildings, just fields, bleak in their sameness, and no sign of those mountains.

Old houses make me self-conscious. I knew no one could see me, but somewhere there were eyes. I made the bed, straightening the frayed satin edge of the blanket, plumping up the vintage pillow – admiring the frugality of rich people – and I did these things as though a camera were embedded in the ceiling's cornice.

Everything now was performative: I was *brushing my hair, dressing neatly*. Then I was *closing the door quietly behind me* and *walking down the grand staircase*, through the house's formal area to the servants' quarters. A line of bells was still mounted on the wall, showing where in the front of the house the help were required: CONSERVATORY, DINING ROOM, YELLOW ROOM, BEST BEDROOM, DAY NURSERY. Here at the back, extra dingy rooms seemed to have been added as the household's staff multiplied, although as far as I could see, only one person was now in residence.

In the kitchen, Alexander had washed last night's dishes, stacking them neatly by the sink. Above the sink a window looked onto an orchard. Long grass grew between twisting, bare trees. To the glass he'd stuck a note:

> *Checking cattle – back by midday. Make yourself at home.*
> *AC*

So he hadn't been able to face me. It was hardly a surprise. If I'd been quicker-witted I'd have realised the morning after was always going to be fraught. Sustaining the intensity of our city appointments was near impossible. So what had I expected?

A dirty weekend, actually, for which I'd be paid.

I opened a door of the refrigerator: vegetables in the salad drawer, and a half-dozen bottles of champagne. I opened the other door: a freezer filled with labelled containers, each one holding meat. An inventory was taped to the inside of the door listing dates and contents, as though some mad creature – with two brains, three loins, seven hoofs – had just been vanquished. Alexander had drawn little boxes next to each item; some were ticked.

The clock struck and I jumped before laughing to cover my nerves, *laughing loudly like there was no problem*. It was nine o'clock. He was not supposed to be back for a few hours, but listening, I now heard something else. A door slamming?

'Alexander?' I called.

There was no answer.

Peering out of the kitchen, down a thin corridor, I called again. 'Hello?'

The entrance hall was empty. Through a clear patch of the front door's stained-glass panel I made out the circle of pebbled driveway – only Alexander's car was parked there. Whatever I'd heard must have been some corner of the house heaving with age. I turned the front door handle and cursed aloud. It was locked.

There was no key in the door, on the ledge of the glass, or anywhere else that I could see. Irritation washed through me, and when it had passed I could feel something else – my heartbeat.

I walked back to the servants' quarters. Past the kitchen, I found a cloakroom. Here there was another door. It was battered, finger-stained; the handle moved but would not open.

It was sick, I know, but I thought of my wrists being tied.

On one of our first meetings, we were in the lavish bedroom

of retirees who were moving permanently to a coastal property. Standing by their French provincial bed, Alexander took off his tie and weaved it nervously through his hands. 'Have you had a busy day?'

I'd been uploading photographs of different properties to the agency website. 'It was okay.'

The tie was navy with a print of light blue squares. 'Many sales?'

Not wanting to talk, I held out my wrists.

'Oh,' he said. 'Yes, of course.'

I waited while he fumbled with the knot. 'I'd have thought a farmer would be good at this.'

'Sorry, nearly there.' Alexander glanced up; he was genuinely trying to get it right. 'Perhaps I, I should tie you *to* something.'

The carved bed head had no rails. Across the room was a Louis Quatorze-style chair, and if I lay on the carpet the smooth bedspread would stay undisturbed. These were the shortcuts I was still learning. (After taking a shower together, I'd found myself saying goodbye at the door only to have to return and painstakingly wipe each drop of water off the glass cubicle.)

I positioned myself, wrists next to the chair leg.

As he bent over me – leaning as he might over a sheep that needed tethering – I supposed we were both thinking how bad the other was at this game. I was admonishing myself for not quite taking control, or not taking control in quite the right way. It was supposed to be the person paying whose hands were tied, wasn't it? And obviously it would have been better to undress before being disabled. Very politely Alexander went about removing which of my clothes he could, carefully folding them so they wouldn't crease, and then he did the same with his own (and socks were never sexy things). He came down to me in a teetering fall, rigid, like a toppling statue. There was the slow summoning of conviction. He seemed too straight to leave me tied up but I lay surrendered, focusing on the oriental wallpaper patterned with a little peak-hatted, plaited man in a pagoda. His own precious piece of real estate.

But the locked door – I stood staring at it.

Had Alexander 'forgotten' I was here?

Turning, my footsteps echoed with a confidence I did not feel. Despite the grime and bits of comedy, this house still knew its power. And all the decoration – the friezes, the plasterwork – seemed an elaborate distraction, not unlike my host's manners, the ornament leading you further from the actual man. He'd left me no option but to snoop around.

Off the grand entrance hall were two rooms: the dining room and the drawing room.

The air in the drawing room had a kind of shimmer to it, a live quality that I figured was dust. After inheriting the house Alexander had evidently changed nothing. Every object was in its pedantic place, including the squat couch upon which, the night before, I'd started to undress. All the cushions were now perfectly straight, their geometry punitive.

A bird made a call like a whip – I glanced out the window.

The garden went mute, nothing moved.

When I turned back to the still room, the kookaburras and cockatoos, frozen on branches in their glass case, seemed too alert. I looked again out at the garden, where I presumed the birds had once lived, then back to the uncanny décor, which felt as alive as the birds. That was the way of antiques – a chair picked up some force from all the people who had sat in it, a vase from the hands that had touched it. They carried absence. The absence of those who'd previously used the objects in this room was palpable. People were needed to keep them under control.

I walked across the hall to the dining room.

Above the fireplace hung the portrait of Alexander's great-great-grandfather – mutton-chop sideburns, rosacea, a death stare. You don't need looks to start a dynasty.

Around him framed sepia photographs gave an Australian history lesson: colonial prosperity to Edwardian dissipation. After the old man did the hard work his progeny were mostly at leisure – at shoots, hunts, tennis games, balls. *Arabella Presented at Court,* read a hand-written inscription under one picture. I guessed this thin-lipped woman in a tiara and elaborate gown was Alexander's great-grandmother. *Unpacking the Rocking Horse*: her six lace-collared children stood in a pile of straw surrounding the carved horse. *Fun for All!:* two young men in three-piece suits spun a skipping rope for long-faced girls in white dresses and hats, the house rising up in the background, watching. Then a series of a man playing polo, and this same man riding an elephant alongside a laughing woman – both having a grand time as the money slips away.

I imagined Alexander returning to this house after visiting me, letting himself in and having all his pedigree shine back at him. Each room would be cool on hot days, a balm against whatever aspects of our meeting left him uneasy. At any moment we could have been caught in one of those apartments by whoever else had possession of a key. But he'd got away with it. He'd transgressed and returned to this life unscathed, no one any the wiser.

Down the corridor to the right of the staircase, I found a room Alexander must have used as his office, a large leather-lined desk at its centre. Facing the door were tall filing cabinets marked TAX/ACCOUNTING, CATTLE, SHEEP, EXPORT/ASIA, EXPORT/ARABIA, and arranged on the desk in careful stacks were account books, lists of forthcoming cattle sales, cropping records, spreadsheets on exchange rates, a calculator. There was also a newish computer set to a weather satellite; swirling cloud patterns moved across the screen.

Along one wall were high bookcases full of volumes with leather bindings now turned to suede. I moved a few steps forward to inspect this library, as if the books were my true interest. He seemed to know a little about a lot, and I tried to guess which ones he had read. Even the newer books were at least fifty years old. His father's perhaps? The various titles on cattle and sheep breeding included the huge tome *Merino*. This was near Margaret Mead's *Coming of Age in Samoa*, while on the shelves out of reach was Churchill's *A History of the English-Speaking Peoples*, and, detailing the locals' more recent past, a lot of books about mining by someone called Blainey.

I stood staring at the spines.

I was in his house, in his element. Around me was every clue to who Alexander Colquhoun was and yet I felt my picture of him disassembling.

The few posh boys I had known at close quarters seemed to have a vacancy about them. They were nice, dull, ground-down souls. Although maybe their class stopped them opening their treasure vaults to girls like me. Alexander was their antipodean cousin. Surely his blankness was just blankness, not a screen for something else.

'I've never been with a prostitute before,' he said after our bondage session, as if apologising for the awkwardness.

I've never been a prostitute before, I thought. The word itself seemed to make me one.

'Often I feel I don't quite know who you are,' he went on.

The owners were due back any minute, and to palm him off I asked lightly, 'Do we ever truly know the other?' I was whoever he found me to be; certainly I'd given up on finding myself. It looked like being just more of the same. Channelling this other person – this prostitute within – seemed far more rewarding. But now, standing in his study, I saw my problem: I'd been subsumed in my role, and this had been a kind of idiocy, leaving me deaf and blind to the clues my client handed out.

I picked up his appointment book. Page after page where apparently he saw no one, then a small 'L' on the days we had met alongside the addresses of various properties. I opened bills he'd folded into the book's pages, receipts for the farming chemicals Omethoate or Trifluralin or Ester 680, scanning them for some sign. Who are *you*? I picked up his account books, looking down the neat columns, as though I were capable of understanding any irregular expenditure. *Who are you?* I even started riffling through a pile of tractor brochures, wanting to shake some fruit from the high branches to identify the tree. *Often I feel I don't quite know who you are . . .*

Why did I not know? I did not know because I had not bothered to find out. That was the truth. People think sex is a good way to understand another person, but it's like studying someone's shadow to determine how reliable or smart or confident or sincere or knowing or dangerous they are. Alexander seemed 'normal enough' – whatever gauge that was – and I hadn't particularly wanted to get into his parents having neglected him, or how he'd roamed around the farm like a feral prince until the day he went to one of *those* boarding schools, one he'd hated.

He had hinted at these things, the barest details of his story, during our assignations, although I half felt I could have predicted them. I could have told you there was something about him which other children would not have liked. Stiff, cerebral, he'd have been bullied and would have annoyed those bullies further by reacting with hauteur, by not seeming to particularly care he was being harassed. And I don't know why, but I imagined the harassment was in keeping with the public-school model. Older boys walking past younger boys' rooms, slowly dragging a cane across the doors, and the younger ones peeing themselves as they waited to see if they were about to be beaten. It put a kink in their tastes.

After some false starts, after I had a better idea of what Alexander wanted, the two of us got together in places made as nice and inviting as they could be for sale. On some sectional couch a couple had laboured over choosing together, or hoisted on their marble kitchen bench, the knife block within easy reach, the uptight, careful Mr Colquhoun became a different man. Or rather different men, and this seemed the perfect arrangement. I might have a craving to see him – whoever he was – and inevitably there'd be the call. Past a certain cursory tour of each new property, I figured we had no need to pretend we'd come together for any other reason than desire. Desire and its most creative expression. Every step of a staircase, for instance, could offer some startling new position, or angle, or matching of parts. A plate-glass window was a kind of brace and vertiginous stage (one squirt of Windex and the city views were again uninterrupted). As far as I was concerned we were discovering the meaning of modern architecture, giving it a purpose. And then there was the money, the aphrodisiacal cash waiting at the end.

I opened a drawer of Alexander's desk. I knew it would be no help, but I was doing it anyway, to satisfy those watching. People always put what they want to hide towards the back and I went there first. Old cheque stubs, business cards. I could feel my heart beating faster. A second drawer: white paper, blue ballpoint pens, perfectly sharpened pencils.

I opened the last drawer: it was full of correspondence. A neat pile of envelopes all with his name in an old-fashioned script – *Mr Alexander Colquhoun*. I weighed the letters in my hands, wondering if I should read them.

A sound, or what I imagined was a sound.

I returned the letters and closed the drawer.

This moment felt too familiar. I was standing in a stranger's house, looking through his things. In the past four months this had become standard. I would be naked, boiling a vendor's kettle to make post-coital tea. And as I drank that tea, or helped myself to a green apple from a careful arrangement meant for display, perhaps Alexander would be wearing the vendor's bathrobe.

Now, looking again at the computer screen, I felt a hit of self-revulsion.

Suddenly I was conscious of being beneath this sky moving in colour-coded fronts across the weather radar. I was beneath Alexander's clouds, his ozone, his atmosphere. With a rush of vertigo, I sensed my imprisonment.

In the entrance hall, I tried the door handle again even though I knew it was locked. The reality of this situation struck me with a mixture of dread – fierce, immediate, intuitive – and something close to hilarity; a kind of sick humour, a humour that made me feel sick. Of course this would be happening, I thought, of course it would. Here was the punishment for my own transgressions. I was now utterly in a stranger's house, and this time I did not have a key.

Laughing while feeling nauseous, I pictured a brothel's panic button – the lesson I hadn't learnt – and again I tried the handle, and again. At school I'd laugh whenever the teachers reprimanded me, and my nerves came across as insouciance, and the teachers would get angrier, and the absurdity made me keep going – just as it did now. *Of course this would happen.* I pulled at the handle in case I had misunderstood its mechanism. No.

Had Alexander calculated no one would know where I was?

In the dining room French doors, sheathed in their moth-eaten velvet, led to the veranda. I pulled aside the curtains to try each door handle and found every one of them also locked. Last night's silver candlestick was still in the centre of the table, and just as I pictured myself smashing a window I noticed a little hook partly hidden behind the curtains, upon which hung a key. I stuck the key in the keyhole. Pushing out onto the veranda I took in lungfuls of fresh air.

I rushed towards the driveway where the Mercedes, Alexander's maroon sedan, was parked. I went to the driver's side, thinking even as I did so, You're overreacting. There's no real problem; stay calm. My fingers on the cold handle, I attempted to open the door. It wouldn't, of course. And what if it had? I wasn't exactly going to hotwire the car. I looked around. Just garden. A still and vast garden.

A bird flew overhead and the day was so silent I heard its beating wings.

Spreading in meticulous symmetry from the house were the planting beds and pathways that had once been carefully designed and landscaped. They were now in disrepair but I found the picture oddly reassuring.

Upon the lawn were trees set out like characters in a play: an elm, a chestnut, an oak, all sharing in the house's air of regret, their canopies having fallen – and that was it. The plants were from an English garden. I could have been standing in a park back at home, one that no one visited. It was completely empty except for three or four wooden benches discretely placed under the trees, and birds – the wrong birds. Grey parrots with hot-pink bellies strutted across the damp grass.

A wind came through and swung the empty branches. Then the stillness again, everything waiting. The view from my bedroom window had shown that beyond the garden was flat farmland as far as the eye could see. This was a little lesson on infinite-point perspective — I was standing right under those swirling electronic clouds surrounded now by vanishing points.

socks, his lips parched, his eyes remote – the king returned to his castle. I'd thought he might hold last night against me, but he came and stood very close.

'Have you been waiting for a certain someone?'

I realised I always looked up at him, and he down at me. 'Yes.'

'I like that,' Alexander said. 'I like the idea of you here in the house, waiting. Did you miss me?'

I nodded.

'But only a little?' He measured some reluctance, shaking his head. 'I missed you a great deal.' His smile was gallant, bemused. 'And what, may I ask, have you been doing?'

My heart was still uneasy in my chest. 'Not a lot.'

'Relaxing, perhaps?' He waited.

I waited too, not wanting him to know I was shaken by his little play with the locked doors.

'Forgive me for leaving you here alone. I've had a busy morning.' At the sink he got himself water, and the glass appeared fragile in his hands. His right knuckle was cut up, scratched. 'A ewe got trapped,' he explained, when he saw me notice. 'An elderly ewe in an elderly fence.' Putting the glass down, he walked to the fridge and took out three plastic containers. A picnic basket rested on the bench top, and he put the containers into it. 'Liese, I thought I might take you on a drive.'

'Where to?'

'Well, if you wouldn't mind, the national park, although first I'd like to show you the farm, would that suit?' He looked like a hard man but the way he spoke could be almost effete. 'You'll need some different clothes. Please, come with me.'

From the cloakroom's bluestone walls hung rows of oilskin coats, stiff with grime. Underneath the coats were compartments full of riding helmets and work clothes and old boots covered in ancient dust. Alexander reached into one compartment and handed me a heavy khaki woman's shirt, and trousers. Taking them, I paused.

The gun I should have known would be in the house rested against the wall. A double-barrelled thing.

Alexander watched me hesitate. 'Would you prefer I turn around?'

I shrugged.

After last night there were no coy flourishes, no suggestive moves, and as he watched me strip, his expression was wry but appraising, as if he were doing sums on my condition: the muscle and flesh and skin tone. I stood in my underwear, expensive lace contrivances I'd selected for the role, goose-pimpled from the cold stone under my feet, trying not to tremble while holding his gaze.

'You seem nervous. Is something wrong?'

'I'm freezing.' The moment broke, and I hurried to cover myself.

His eyebrow went up in a little parody of concern. 'You're sure there's no problem?'

Mentally I weighed the thick envelope of cash upstairs. 'What could possibly be wrong?'

Alexander's expression gave nothing away. He chose a jacket, a sheen of wear around the collar and wrists, and placed it over my shoulders. A perfume then of lavender and dog. My arms through the sleeves, he half lifted me around and carefully fastened each button. In such a small space he took up most of it; his face was in my face. I hadn't seen him unshaven before.

Turning, he checked what I kept glancing at. 'Don't worry, it's not loaded,' he said. 'Oh, and by the way, there's a trick to this door.' He leaned his shoulder against the heavy timber while turning the handle, both pushing and pulling. It opened with a heave, the glass panes shuddering. 'Although I might start locking it.'

Outside, the back of the house showed its workings: extensions, erected through the decades, jutted out in different styles as if the house itself had periodically mutated. Stacked against the bluestone walls was an assortment of gardening paraphernalia; a project involving the parts of an elaborate concrete fountain seemed to have been abandoned.

'How to put this?' Alexander stopped to growl at the barking dogs. He was carrying the picnic basket, which he now fixed at a distance to them on the open bed of the truck. 'I mean, I don't want to sound dramatic, but some odd things have been happening.'

'What kind of odd things?'

He squinted. 'Someone's been writing to me.'

The letters I'd found in his desk drawer. 'Writing things you don't want to read?'

'Correct.' He opened the truck's passenger door and I climbed in.

The vinyl dashboard was equipped with a CB radio and a large knife in a worn leather sheath. It was covered with dried mud. So was the steering wheel, and the floor, and all the upholstery.

He closed the door and I watched for him in the rear-view

mirror. Did his slumped posture mark a bad mood?

'Anyway.' Settling into the driver's seat, he smiled. 'I should have introduced you to Zinc and Florence.' As the engine rattled to life, the dogs moved around on the tray, straining against their chains.

I put on my seatbelt. He did not put on his. We were closer now than I really wanted us to be.

Alexander steered the truck through an old carriage gateway, marked by two tall bluestone columns. The garden ended abruptly and I stared with barely seeing eyes at vast tawny fields separated by cypresses that acted as windbreaks. It was a relief to be out of the house, but I wasn't feeling myself, and nor did I feel like the character I'd been hired to play. Around us, his land seemed to stretch uninterrupted in every direction.

'You're very quiet,' he said.

'Where are the mountains?' I asked.

'Which way is the sun?'

'I have no idea.'

'It's behind us – north-east, so we're driving south-west.' Alexander took us down another dirt road, stopping at an iron gate. He waited, expecting me to climb out and open it.

I did not move.

On his side of the truck, in the distance, was a herd of black cows.

'Okay, allow me.' Giving in, I stepped into the wind and cold. My shoes were not designed for the mud underneath them.

'Be careful where you walk,' he called over the engine.

'Why?'

'A cow calved by the gatepost.'

I looked at him.

'Placenta,' he added, straight-faced.

At the next paddock we adopted the same procedure, with me taking tentative strides to open and close the gates. This paddock looked just like the last. Cows and their calves stood in various configurations. In the paddock after that were a dozen bulls, blue-black with yellow eyes full of disdain. And after that, sweet-faced ewes, then rams, formally dressed with their horns on.

As we kept driving Alexander didn't bother with any tour narrative, and I couldn't have absorbed one anyway. Something about these scenes shocked me: I suppose I'd imagined animals in bonnets and knickerbockers, leading chaste Beatrix Potter lives under the nose of a lusty, distracted farmer. The reality shut me up. These creatures stared back at us with silent reproach. They looked resigned. Resigned to living in a paddock for a few years until someone hit them on the head. Nothing to do but eat grass, have babies, and stand there, waiting.

It was a revelation that Alexander spent his days with these animals like this, the days he didn't spend with me. Each new paddock furthered my sense of the land and his labours multiplying underneath us. The elements were communicating things I couldn't understand, and our silence deepened.

He was showing me his country, as he'd promised in the letter. And what was my side of the bargain? Was I meant to be scared, or in awe, or manufacturing an air of infatuation? From one angle, if you weren't frightened of Alexander – and my fear was losing its grip as I slipped back into taking him for granted – and if you liked his style of looks, his brooding, and his substantial landholdings, the task of seeming to fall for him wasn't too difficult. Why did he even need to pay someone to spend the weekend with him? I hoped the reason was that he liked paying, just as I liked being paid. An affair is such a nebulous thing; one never knows exactly where it begins or ends, or where one is in it from one day to the next. Here the terms were clear. There were rules and therefore definition.

'I suppose you've had many girlfriends?'

The question surprised him. 'A few.'

'But never Miss Right?'

'She has been elusive.'

I smiled as though I understood. 'So, after you finished high school you came back to the farm?'

'Yes.'

'Did you go backpacking first?'

'Go what?'

'Don't all Australians do that?' A nervous laugh.

He kept staring straight ahead. 'I had a lot of responsibility from a young age. After my father died, this place was mine to solve . . . There were problems at the start.' His jaw tightened. 'Serious financial problems as well as other things I had to deal with.'

I felt resentment coming up from the ground like it was a kind of crop.

'How did you know what to do here? I mean, had your dad taught you to be a farmer?'

'Hardly.' Alexander's tone was dismissive. 'His generation

weren't interested in getting their hands dirty. He was raised to be a gentleman, sent to Cambridge, and in his head at least he never came back. He inherited twenty thousand acres from his father, who'd been a wastrel. I inherited seven thousand . . . No, there were no helpful lessons. He hated farming.'

'You weren't close?'

'My father was never here, and he wasn't the type to write – not even a postcard.'

We came to some thirty cows standing close together in a yard. Each one had a red cross marked on its flank. 'None of these girls are in calf,' Alexander told me matter-of-factly. 'They're on their last chance. One more service and then they'll have to be culled.'

'How many . . . services have they had?'

'One.'

Each cow looked so vulnerable – each one with a different face, different features – some standing primly, others dejected, their legs sagging. Their voices were doleful or insistent, and nothing much like the *moo* noises nursery children learn. *Yes*, they seemed to call, *we hate it here too*.

'Did you ever think of not coming back to the farm? Of, say, taking a different job?'

Alexander sighed. 'Perhaps I'd have studied law. I'm interested in people and what they do, in different ideas of right and wrong.'

'You could have sold this place and done law.'

'No, I couldn't,' his voice earnest. 'I could never have done that.'

There was another silence.

'Liese,' he said, 'we'll have lunch shortly, but first I've got to move these ladies into another paddock. Would you mind unchaining the dogs?'

They were on the back barking and straining at their leads.

He cocked his head to the open window, growled, *'Sitdown!'* The barking stopped. He turned back to me. 'They'll be fine.'

A gust of cold hit my face as I got out of the truck. The dogs had golden eyes and gleaming fur and sharp teeth, but they sat quietly. I swallowed as I reached around to unclip one then another chain.

'Getawayback!'

They leapt off the tray into the grass.

Alexander drove after them, instructing the dogs in shouts of 'Pushemup!' or 'Goaround!' and the occasional angry 'Getoutofit!'

I pulled the jacket he'd lent me closer. This farm was as bleak and as dun-coloured as home – the fens with some gum trees. On the Norfolk flatlands the wind was personal – trying to get into *your* brain, to make *you* give up. Here it felt no different.

The dogs drove the cows – their soft faces concerned, their lumpy bodies jostling – through the gate.

I closed the steel bolt on them.

Returning to the truck, I was again dodging cowpats and the deeper mud – something about this farce and the way Alexander sat in the driver's seat, his shoulders slumped, made me think: You're crazy, this man is no one to be scared of. He's a farmer who wishes he wasn't a farmer. Deeply lonely – like most who need to pay for company – and in flight from his own melancholy.

Shivering from the wind, I settled back into the passenger seat. Perhaps the two of us weren't so dissimilar: we were both less than comfortable in our own skin, both had taken pleasure pretending to be people we weren't.

As we drove off, Alexander turned to me, his smile full of expectation.

Just smile back, I thought, try to be pleasant and get the cash at the end.

The only problem was part of me was starting to feel bad about taking this man's money. I liked being paid. I liked it very much. After our first meeting, when to my surprise he'd agreed to my higher fee, I found myself making constant calculations of how many hours we'd need to screw before I could pay off my creditors. Debt filled my days with arithmetic. Each note seemed a surrogate for our adventure, and as a means of savouring the experience, I treated them with extra care. The cash was alive when I slipped it into my wallet, and still alive when I checked it the next morning. Finally I was saving money. However, the envelope hidden back in the house now felt like punishment as well as reward. Alexander's sadness seeped through his clothes, and I was not entirely convinced my fee was well earned, or even, looking around, that he could afford it. But I was trapped by the cash the way one can be trapped by guilt – despite my reservations about keeping his money, I doubted I could actually leave that much of it behind.

'My father never understood the basics – that good-quality stock is the first priority,' Alexander was telling me. He seemed agitated, as though lecturing me were keeping him from doing something more important. 'You've got to have good bloodlines. I try to conserve the old, well-regarded bloodlines, but also mix things. You see the vigour of a hybrid plant?' He nodded for me. 'You want the same in an animal. The purebred is fine, but breeding too pure you get weakness.'

In the distance emerged a cloud of dust: an identical white utility truck was driving towards us, and at the sight of another person, a smile crept over my face.

The driver held his arm up in a wave as he abruptly turned his truck down a different dirt track.

'Is that a neighbour?' I asked.

Alexander shook his head. 'That's the station manager leaving. I've given him the long weekend off. No, breeding is an art,' he went on. 'In the wild, animals sort themselves out, but on a farm you need to oversee it.' He glanced at me and winked. 'Basically I'm always looking for the perfect cross.'

Other than a narrow rust-red dirt track, the land belonging to Alexander's nearest neighbour – the national park – had been left uncleared. Out the truck windows there was chaos on either side, the vegetation dense and scrappy. We rushed past bursts of brilliant yellow wattle, bushes with bristling pod-like extrusions, and bulbous pigmy trees erupting in countless long green spikes – plants all designed in a radical workshop. Nowhere in England would you move so fast from pastoral land into vast, wild disorder.

'Emu,' Alexander called, hitting the dashboard. Further down the track the creature's feathered rump and legs disappeared into the shrub. 'I told you I'd show you the real Australia!'

'Thank you . . . I'd love to see a koala.'

'You never know.'

The mountains were closer now, close on all sides. We must have been high up and above the tree-line; sometimes I could make out the detail of the boulders and vegetation on the rock walls. 'Did you come here as a child?' I was trying to be kinder to him.

'Occasionally.'

'You must have favourite places?'

'There are a few.'

We turned a sharp corner and Alexander parked by a solitary road sign, badly buckled. Near it the gum trees had black boughs.

'A fire ripped through here a few years ago,' he said.

'That's sad.'

'Why?' Leaving the dogs chained to the back of the truck, he untied the picnic basket and lifted it off. 'Most of these trees were probably having the time of their lives. They're pyromaniacal, even their leaves are doused in propellant.' He sniffed forcefully, the way boxers do. 'This whole ecosystem is predicated on everything burning.'

We walked for a few minutes until we came to a stretch of water framed all around by violet-coloured mountain peaks. At first the sight was overwhelming. The water, flat as a mirror, held each purple-blue fold and crag – and also the clouds. Otherworldly and completely unpeopled, this place reminded me of a location in a children's fantasy story. There should have been an imaginary amphibian coming ashore, sorcerers lurking behind the escarpment. But we were alone.

Alexander positioned the picnic basket near the water's edge. He pulled out of it a tartan rug which he spread with an air of careful urgency.

'This is extraordinary. It's beautiful here.'

'Make yourself comfortable, Liese.'

'Really,' I said, touching his arm as I sat down. 'It's like nothing I've seen before.'

Pleased, he continued unpacking the basket's surreal contents. On china crockery he laid out a complicated assortment of sandwiches and fruit and cheese like religious offerings. Kneeling, half in prayer himself, he handed me a linen napkin. 'I hope you're hungry.'

'What a feast,' I said, 'how delicious' – these platitudes the wrong scale for a place like this. Birdsong was in the foreground with frogs, their rattling as rhythmic as a chain gang, layered underneath. Everything around us seemed to be humming. The *aliveness* of the wind and the water and the plants and the animals combined in a way that made the compass in my head start to whirl. Go with this, I urged myself. Soon you'll leave Australia and this will be what you've seen of it. But the silence between us had a new quality. We sat eating the gourmet sandwiches, staring at the lake. Glancing over at him, I smiled, although in truth the effort he'd gone to filled me with unease. This scene, so idyllic, had the scent of ambush.

Under a napkin in the basket was a bottle of champagne. 'Shall we have a drink?' I sounded too eager.

'In a moment.' Straight-backed and straight-faced, he asked solemnly, 'Liese, what do you most want in life?'

'Food, shelter . . .' My fingers holding the plate felt slightly numb with cold.

'Happiness?'

I hated these sorts of conversations. 'Yes, life's happier that way, isn't it?'

He frowned, as if deciding. 'I don't often feel comfortable enough to show people all this.' There was a pause. 'I wouldn't have imagined that with our . . . our differences in background and experience this could happen. Thank you.'

'You're welcome.' I didn't want to follow his point.

'No, really, thank you.'

The wind sent a shiver over the water's surface; briefly it turned reptilian, scaled. Alexander was courting me, but the problem was he did not seem to be acting.

'I feel I can be myself with you,' he said.

'I'm very glad.' *But who exactly would that be?*

Now he put his arm around my already tense shoulders. As I sat still I could hear him breathing. I could hear my own dumb breath. *This is all an act. You are being paid to be romantic,* I told myself, *to facilitate some fantasy.* The professionals called this The Girlfriend Experience. I'd read about it online. An escort acts like an idealised girlfriend: giving backrubs, laughing at stupid jokes, not checking her watch while fellating. (And in special cases, according to the chat-sites, allowing BBBJ: a bareback blow job; DATY: dinner at the Y; and crime-scene action: sexual activity during menstruation.)

The problem was I wasn't used to being a girlfriend, anyone's girlfriend, and so I didn't really know what to be faking. I would go on a date, even a series of dates, and soon enough have the feeling – like running into an old acquaintance – that this new romance would not work out. Before long we'd be sitting in a restaurant finding we didn't have much to say.

Even at the best of times I knew I came across as disconnected. I was there, but not there; often more aroused by the thought of intercourse than by the act itself, presenting my body at the outset so as to say, You can have this, but no more. Then, after the physical contact was over, something shattered. Almost immediately the man beside me seemed to be covered in tiny blemishes, and he was a little overweight, and painted with sweat, and he was *there*. Right there. I would have to try to be sensitive, acting as if I didn't already wish to be alone. The way some men unburdened themselves after sex could mortify me; the way they suddenly revealed their most gruesome vulnerabilities, their need for reassurance, affirmation, eye contact – when all I wanted was to roll over and forget they even existed. Their neediness making me think, I should be getting paid for this.

Alexander's arm grew heavier on my shoulders.

'Can you imagine staying longer in Australia?'

'Oh, well it's a lovely place,' I told him, sensing that would not be enough. 'There's wonderful food, very fresh produce.' That's what everyone said. I picked up a fat, fleshy date upon which he'd plastered camembert. 'And people are so friendly.'

'Good, I'm glad you've found that.'

Australians walked down the street grinning at each other, a bunch of lovely sunny idiots that no one wanted to upset. Everybody else took turns having wars and economic catastrophes to spare them the trouble.

'But,' I was swallowing, 'I think I'd miss England.'

'We have better weather.'

'Yes, it's usually a lot warmer.'

'Less crowded.'

'Out here it certainly is.'

He shifted position. 'How do you find the countryside?'

'The countryside?' I finally laughed. 'Is that what you'd call it?'

Alexander looked impatient. 'What I'm trying to ask is, do you respond to the land?'

I had to stop my chuckling. 'It's fine. I mean, it's beautiful, of course.' Here the beauty was severe. The fire had come right to the edge of the water. Not that this lake brought respite. Seconds earlier I'd seen an eagle take off, and every smaller bird perched nearby try to fly out of range. 'I just don't know much about it.'

'About nature?'

'Yes,' I admitted. 'I suppose I'm denatured.'

'I think that's very sad.' He took his arm from my shoulders, reaching I hoped for the champagne. 'But it can grow on you.' The bottle stayed untouched.

'Are there people out here? Any . . . community?' I asked. 'You must get lonely.'

'Do I seem lonely?'

'No, no, of course not.' I had to avoid sounding like I thought he was desperate. 'I just mean it's very isolated, and that could get to a person if they weren't –' my head to one side, coquettish, flailing – 'as strong as you are.'

'I like it.' He bit into a sandwich.

'Well, as I said, it's beautiful . . . *Do* you have friends nearby?'

'Oh,' he waited until he'd finished eating, 'sometimes I see other members of the district's so-called grand families. But to be honest, they bore me.' His laugh carried a small sneer. 'They see me as an outsider. I haven't married my second cousin.' He picked up a stone and was set to skip it over the flat water, then dropped it. 'God, why are we even talking about them?'

Leaning across, Alexander very carefully took my face in his hands. His hands that appeared to be trembling. 'Liese, I've put a lot of thought into what I'm about to say.' He swallowed hard, glancing up at the sky. 'I want to ask you —'

'Look!'

I'd had to cut him off and fortunately from behind a bank of reeds there emerged a black swan – a cool, poised dream-creature; its gleaming neck twisted like a periscope and was almost a separate entity. At that moment, this bird seemed a maquette, the prototype for all the kitsch ornaments and figurines I'd ever seen – objects of worship that now made sense. 'How magnificent!'

Alexander exhaled loudly. 'Some farmers think they're terrible pests. They eat crops, graze on pasture grasses, bog up the ground.'

Looking at him I felt the heaviness of his expectations. Need was coming off him, but not the type I could fulfil.

'A lot of people imagine swans mate for life. But actually, no.' He almost sounded bitter. 'No, scientists have proven one in six cygnets are illegitimate, if that term means anything in the natural world . . .' His voice trailed off.

'So they do mate for life, they're just unfaithful?'

'You might say one cancels out the other.'

'Anyone can make mistakes.'

His face darkened. 'Yes, they can, but they shouldn't.'

The swan leaned forward as if standing, and ran along the surface of the lake. Its neck was now straight and at the barest angle to the water, its wings like white-edged propellers.

'The male really has to court his mate. It's very formal.' Alexander was distracted by the chance to deliver another lesson. 'She flattens herself on the water, he spreads his wings right over her, pinions her neck with his bill and then it all starts. Although it depends on the female being,' he chose the right word, '*co-operative.*'

Usually, I was the one who got things going between us. I gave him some signal and then it unfolded.

Here, by the water, there was a sexual element to being beyond anyone's gaze, and, I had to concede, to being in nature.

I leaned closer, and put my mouth on his.

I wanted him to give in to me so we could return to the part of the story I understood.

He smelled of farm and I remembered this scent on my skin when we were together, his body against the towel, indenting someone's bedspread – or once, another time outside, someone's daybed. With the sun in his eyes he was as vulnerable then as he ever was, the apple of his neck exposed yet his expression still inscrutable. I was on top, trying to make his face change, to make him show something. How to persuade him to lose control before I did? Often there was an elemental fight taking place between us, the role of prey switching without warning. He might be lying on his back and then, within seconds, bending over my body, long arms and wrists and hands disabling me in a heartbeat. And sometimes then we would talk about my made-up past. I'd tell him stories about the things I'd never done.

Now Alexander held me very tight, pinning my arms to my sides, keeping me in place. At first I thought it was a mode of foreplay – his inhibitions a come-on – and I wrestled, attempting to arouse him, to get him to open his mouth. I needed to taste our game behind what now felt like reality, not the reality behind the game. But nothing in his manner told me he was playing, and when I stopped resisting he did not let me go. Around us was the buzzing and dinning of a million creatures doing their wild things. His grip was hard. Last night he'd just seemed weary or not in the mood; now, in his rejection of me, I detected actual menace.

As my breath grew steady I stared into the distance.

The light had changed over the lake. Rather than being a study in purple, all Middle Earth mauves and indigos, it resembled a black and white photograph – the mountains and sky, and therefore the water, were different tones of grey. This landscape was so full of morphing colours and noises that it occurred to me I was not actually seeing the place. It was all disguise.

'I think I'll ask you my question later,' Alexander said softly, taking his arms off me.

Only the green reeds held their pigment. 'Is this what your land would have once looked like?' I needed to not show any fear.

'Before it was cleared? No, not exactly. The plains below were similar to parks. It was grasslands and gum trees.'

'How did your ancestor first find it?'

'An Aboriginal guide was employed to show him.'

'He just took it?'

'What's your point?'

'Nothing,' I said vaguely.

Why was I provoking him? What did *I* care?

Alexander was already repacking the basket. The half-eaten picnic looked spoiled on the plates – a second meal that had not worked – and scraping the leftovers into a container, he had a private, tight air about him. 'Well, here it is,' he said, without glancing up. 'The bush.'

'Do you know what happened to the Aboriginal guide?' I persisted.

He fixed shut the basket's clasps. 'He lived a long, happy life under the banner of his Lord Jesus. Is that what you want to hear?'

I didn't answer.

His eyes were bright and hard. 'Liese, we'll go home and have a quiet night, but first I have my surprise for you.' Lifting the basket, he started carrying it towards the truck, walking a few paces ahead. When he reached the dogs they began moving expectantly on their chains. He ignored them and secured the basket again.

I hung behind, contemplating the ground. The nearby trees were twisting, roiling as if trying to break free. At the roots of one of them, I noticed a small maroon cylinder. Then I noticed a second cylinder, or rather a second shotgun cartridge: someone had been hunting here, where the animals drank.

Turning, Alexander saw me registering this. He sighed, but the sigh wasn't tired or unhappy. 'I'd come here when I was a child. Camp, catch yabbies, shoot rabbits and ducks – and never once did I ever see a soul.'

'What would someone shoot now?'

'Perhaps kangaroos which jump the fence and eat his crops.'

I nodded.

He waited. 'You were right, Liese. This *is* one of those places that's special to me. If I'm ever under pressure I come here in my thoughts. I want you to be able to do that too. Do you suppose you will?'

'Yes.' Wind played through the leaves of high branches above us. 'I expect so.'

He was giving me his blue stare. 'The mountains and water are so peaceful. I want you to keep the feeling in your head. To remember it. Okay?'

VI

As we drew closer the house was all windows, reflecting the blankness of the darkening sky. Grey clouds rolled over the glass, camouflaging whatever waited behind it. This building sat in the dusk, expectant and watchful, emitting a low piercing sound. Every nearby tree was alive with bird-din. Hundreds, thousands of them were seething in the branches. They signalled to each other, the garden vibrating with their calls – although more truly the sound seemed to come from the stone walls of the house, from deep inside one of its rooms.

Nature might be a wonderful thing, but if you're not used to it, it's a series of creeping shocks. On the drive back I'd found a cobweb stretching along my seatbelt holster, and I kept brushing a crawling sensation off my shoulder. Alexander stopped for me to open and close the gates. A heavy dew had come down; the steel felt damp to the touch. I tried to resist glancing at my watch. I needed to get away from this man, even for half an hour; I needed to get through the house's back door, and straight up the stairs so as to lock myself in the ruin of the bathroom until I could stand another night with him.

He parked by the rear of the house. Here, a garden bench was on its side, rotten through; broken terracotta pots were stacked against the wall. Briskly he unchained the dogs – they bounded off the truck and followed him, moving like shadows towards the kennels.

'Wait a moment,' Alexander called to me. 'I'd like to show you something.'

I stopped.

He secured the dogs in their concrete shelters, bolting shut the mesh doors, then walked slowly over to me, half smiling. 'This is my favourite time in the garden, Liese.'

Sensing my hesitation, he reached out and clasped my fingers in his. He led me to a fruit tree, one in a gnarled and lichen-covered row.

'So, Exhibit A.' Alexander was trying to sound casual, light-hearted. 'The orchard, as you can see, has become very run-down.'

It didn't seem polite to agree too forcefully. But this was the part of the garden he'd forgotten to mow and the grass bent double under our shoes, forming footprints of dew.

'Half of the trees had crown gall,' he continued, pointing to gaps between the old plantings where the sick trees had been felled; here the ground was raised or else a sapling jutted out of bulging grass. 'My parents were not exactly gardeners. I've been trying to replant this patch and bring it back to life. I try to plant old varieties, often from your part of the world: Gravenstein, Lord Lambourne.' He bit at his bottom lip. 'Just a few weeks ago I put in a Kentish cherry.'

It seemed he was saying all this to avoid what was really on his mind.

'Okay, on to the main attraction.'

He steered me further along a narrow path. Even in the dying light, I could see the adjacent plant beds were now filled with a tangle of shrubs that had survived benign neglect, overgrown succulents and lush weeds.

We walked down stone steps between a pair of empty urns. On the lawn Alexander came up behind me and placed a hand on each shoulder, restraining me with his long thick fingers. I could feel his chest moving against my back each time he exhaled.

'I want you to picture this: Warrowill's garden used to cover eight acres, requiring ten full-time gardeners. Eight acres, Liese, and to your left,' his words slid down my neck, 'say, two hundred metres, were glasshouses growing rare fruits and flowers. To your right,' he moved me suddenly, 'to your right, was a lake – man-made – for which my great-great-grandfather imported white swans to replace the native specimen you so admired.'

He had the key to this magic kingdom and I supposed he was deciding whether I was worthy enough to gain entry. 'Peacocks also roamed the lawns, upon which my great-grandfather, when he took over, added a polo ground and – wait for it – Japanese fish ponds. Can you imagine?' His voice was lovelorn but laced with a subtle anger. 'Wouldn't you give anything to have seen it in its glory?'

I was staring at the unkempt lawn, the ragged hedge.

'It must have been quite something,' I said sincerely.

'Of course, it was easier in those days. After the land had been *assumed . . .*' Alexander paused. 'I mean, the old man did pay a fee, of course.'

A pattern seemed to be emerging. 'Of course.'

'And in return for the fee he was also assigned convicts, which meant free labour.'

'The convicts built the glasshouses?'

'No. In the early days they cleared the land of rocks, erected fences with them. Probably later ex-convicts did the construction. It started to fall away in my grandfather's time, the garden I mean, with crown gall, et cetera. As I've told you, he was a waste of space by all accounts.'

Alexander had taken his hands from my shoulders, but standing beside me he wouldn't meet my eye. We were under a cypress pine, and he was still deciding how best to deal with me. He wiped something off his boot. 'Sometimes I linger in this spot and picture how it would have been.'

'Amazing.' I made myself smile, pulling the coat closer.

Above us, birds rearranged themselves in the dark foliage.

'It's getting quite chilly, Alexander.'

'Then we'll walk faster.' Tilting his head deferentially, he took my hand again and held it tighter. 'Over there, you had the croquet lawn.' He gestured towards more empty grass, another acre of unkempt garden. 'And the tennis court.' He pointed in another direction and I could see there was indeed still a court surrounded by a drooping wire fence. It had no net; in the corner, half covered by a creeper, was the old roller.

'It used to be my ambition to restore this garden to its former glory. Now I think, Fuck it!'

I was as shocked as I would have been at ten: I'd never heard him swear before.

'I think, Spare yourself the heartache,' he continued, 'and replant with natives, that won't need water. Let it all go natural. Because will anyone even notice all the effort? I could spend years getting everything just right, and who'd actually be here to appreciate the achievement?' He fixed on me in a way I didn't like. 'And you? Do you enjoy gardening?'

'No. I'm denatured, remember.'

'That doesn't mean you can't have an opinion about my garden.'

'It's very nice.' I wanted him to let go of my hand.

He stopped, blocked by my indifference. 'Liese, I feel you're not really enjoying yourself.'

Untangling my fingers from his. 'I'm just cold.'

'No, you seem bored.' He shook his head; perhaps he thought he was being tested more than was fair. 'Your other clients must be better company. What do they ask of you?'

It was puzzling but I will admit I felt my temperature rise.

He knew very well what 'they' asked, because I'd told him in detail about a stable of imaginary clients and their varied requirements. It was fine if my stories aroused him – *At first I didn't know what to do. The other twins took turns teaching me* – but it was better not to get into too much detail about the logistics, how the hell these scenarios could ever have happened. Our game worked when neither acknowledged it was a game.

'So tell me what the others *really* ask of you,' he now demanded.

I stared down at the lawn: was I supposed to guess his current fantasy or extend my own? 'A lot of men just want to talk,' I said eventually. It sounded dubious to me, but it was what people always claimed. 'You'd be surprised how many are more lonely than randy . . .' The unfinished sentence might have described him.

'What do they talk about?'

'Their families, their wives,' I added quickly.

Alexander paused, considering this. 'And me? Are you listening to me for the same reason?'

'It's different with you.'

He started walking again in quick strides. His chest out, he was heating up, although not as I had. 'How many other clients have you been seeing alongside me?'

I followed him, uncertain for the first time of the right response.

If he was only playing at being possessive I could confess now to a variety of lovers, making him extract the details very, very slowly whilst in this darkening garden I acted breathless and ashamed. If he was serious, I needed to prove my relative chastity as soon as possible.

'I won't be angry. I just need to know.'

'Alexander, it's sort of confidential.'

'Did any of them try to see you more regularly?'

'Everyone had regulars,' I answered automatically, and despite myself, I smiled slightly, as though I could remember the clients of whom I'd been fond.

'Was there ever a man who became too attached to you? I mean, more than is usual?'

'I suppose some did . . .' I was shivering, and not just from the cold.

'Did they try to see you after hours?'

'If they asked to see me outside work, I'd say no, usually.'

'Usually?'

What was I meant to reply?

'Liese, I know how other men fell for you.' His laugh was bitter. 'I know precisely how they couldn't think or work or sleep.'

I hoped we were both now acting. 'No, you don't —'

'I *do*,' he said sharply. 'Really, I do.'

A narrow entrance had been cut in the hedge. I followed him through the opening – the privet so old it was metres thick – into another garden, set out in a perfect square, planted with rose bushes, perhaps twelve rows by twelve, with violets growing underneath. The roses had all recently been pruned hard, as if the point were really to harvest thorns, and the stubby root of each bush sent out twisting, arthritic shoots, like crossed fingers.

Twice my height, the hedge obscured the trees outside. I felt I was in the centre of a maze. Being here was thrilling. Then, just as quickly it was not: I had a sense – a flash of sense – that I was trapped.

Without speaking, Alexander sat on a garden bench placed along one wall. Behind him, the soft hedge had the uneven sheen of an animal's fur. He was leaning back into the brush, it was giving way to him, and he was staring at me, suddenly beholding a great truth.

'Come and sit,' he called.

'This must be incredible when the roses are in bloom.' I stretched and yawned, trying now to defuse the situation with a little banality. 'It must smell incredible.'

He gestured to the space beside him on the bench.

Past the rows of stunted bushes, I walked towards him.

He was looking up at me with an expression of peculiar intensity. 'Do you have something to tell me?'

Alexander knew before I knew that I was going to call this weekend off, and my reasons spilled out in a sudden, disorganised mess.

'Look, I'm sorry,' I started, taking a seat, 'I just can't do this any more. It's beginning to warp.'

'What is?'

'What was good before.'

'Am I warping, Liese?'

'No, of course not.' Although he was more mercurial than I had realised – and what did it say about me that for four months I'd got off on avoiding the discovery?

I couldn't look him in the eye. 'It's more that I need to stop – how to put this? – selling you myself.' That is actually what this is, I understood sharply, I've been dressing it up as just some erotic escapade, but it *is* a kind of prostitution, accidental prostitution.

'It could be dangerous!' I blurted out. 'I mean, there are con-sequences to doing this that aren't good for either of us. What I'm trying to say, I know clumsily, is it's gone too far. And that's my fault, Alexander, I've taken it too far . . .' Shaking my head. 'We'll still be friends, hopefully,' I said, wishing those lines did not always sound so insincere, wiping at my nose with the back of my hand. I was prepared to give him a fair refund, taking into account the time we'd already spent together, and perhaps then he could just take me to a railway station.

Behind us the privet had that cloying, almost sweet smell of menthol and piss. 'I'm just so sorry,' I said, sniffling, 'but I have to give this job away.'

Alexander's smile was almost innocent. 'Believe it or not, I've been waiting for you to say that.' He was nodding in relieved disbelief. 'Your timing's perfect.'

Only when I saw the small black leather box did I understand.

He handed it to me, and asserting each word said, 'I don't care about your past.'

Inside the box's velvet lining, the ring was antique: a thin platinum band balancing a square-cut diamond. Light: the stone held so much of it, even in the dusk, whole rooms of light.

I glanced up, checking if Alexander was joking, if I could trace any irony, but his face was flushed with a stunned kind of tenderness. The box shook in my hand – did raising the stakes of this game still constitute play?

'Do you like it?'

I could hardly breathe. 'It's beautiful.'

'Then why not try it on?' He gave an awkward chuckle. 'Check if it fits.'

The ease of slipping this ring on my finger, the ease that would follow: my debts taken care of, my family off my back, friends no longer emitting their low vibration of pity, and the grand house – I could renovate it, I could knock down walls and bring it back to life . . . A part of me wanted to slip on that magic ring very much.

'I can't.'

'I think you can.'

Overhead, a skein of birds wavered and then the hedge blocked them. It occurred to me that declining his offer would be easier somewhere it was possible to hail a taxi.

'Put the past behind you,' Alexander said.

I could not tell if he was trying to be funny.

'Liese, let me take it away from you.'

Smiling tightly: 'I don't think I can ask you to do that.'

'Please, stop fighting and put the ring on your finger!' Cheerfully impatient, Alexander now cleared his throat, hushing me despite my silence. 'Don't you see? You don't have to keep running any more.' He was speaking as though to someone else, someone just over my shoulder. As he gazed at this stranger he looked handsome, incredibly handsome – how close a nightmare can be to an exquisite dream. I almost wished I was not so filled with horror.

He said to his stranger, 'I love you. You are not who I would have imagined loving, or who I'd have chosen to love. And yet I find I do.'

'Alexander,' I inhaled, wondering how to frame this, 'you realise I am not actually a prostitute?'

He grinned at me indulgently. 'No?'

'No. Let's be clear. I haven't done this sort of thing before.'

He kept smiling. 'Really?'

'Really!' I laughed; this was all so ludicrous. 'I've never done it before in my life – other than with you.'

His expression did not change.

I tried now to flick some switch, to reach him through gravitas. Speaking slowly, as if explaining things to a child: 'And even then, it was a game – just a game that we both enjoyed, didn't we?'

'A game?'

I nodded.

Alexander paused, thinking. 'But you took my money, didn't you?'

'Yes, but that was only to make things more . . .' I struggled for the right word, '*authentic.*'

'You took my money and I presume you enjoyed spending it? And that enjoyment was also "authentic"? Or do you plan to give it back?'

Beyond the hedged walls, each tree was filled with the shrill music of those thousand birds made invisible by the dusk. Twilight was an encryption. The high walls – like those of a great square box – were now no longer green but the colour of lead, and the dimming sky was folding down, closing over us.

My whole body felt worn out, my marrow cold.

'You can't unmake a whore, Liese. You can't refund the money and undo what you've done.' Alexander winced faintly, lowering himself onto bended knee, his thigh stiff, the thick fabric of his trousers pulling tight. His face was close to my face in the near dark. Firmly he took my hand. He didn't bother proposing again. 'Now,' he said sternly, taking the ring from its box and putting it hard on my finger. 'Now you are mine.'

PART TWO

I

I lay in the darkened room. The ring was on my finger. Its little leather box was on the bedside table. How naïve I'd been, how ridiculously naïve. Of course Alexander would want to save me from my fake past, to exorcise all the different men who hadn't come before him. Of course he would try to sanctify his own lust by using a wedding dress like whitewash . . . I waited on the single bed not even knowing what I was waiting for. Light seeped in from under the door, and above me I traced the outline of a cornice, of a plasterwork ceiling rose. Slowly, manoeuvring my arm free from the blankets, I felt around on the side table for the ring box. The light in the hallway suddenly faded. I was clasping the hard leather weight in my hand, staring into the dark.

If I gave myself up to this man he could make me whomever he wanted me to be – including no one. As his wife I'd never be allowed to unmake myself a whore. The past he would free me from would be my real past; then he would have no need to bother himself with my likes or dislikes, my opinions, my moods, with who I was. He could talk any way he chose, or not at all; expect me to laugh at his jokes, to listen, fascinated, to all his stories. And he could fuck me on demand, whenever, however, he liked, using my body, every part of it, in any way he desired.

Easing off the ring, I put it back inside the little velvet coffin and snapped shut the lid.

After the proposal we'd come in from the hedged garden, Alexander pulling me through the chill of the entrance hall towards the drawing room. Everything vibrated with the surreal – the room's dimensions seemed enlarged, and his hand in mine too fleshy, too alive – and then he was taking me in his arms, or rather taking my hand and placing it upon his shoulder, arranging it there, while he spread his swollen fingers over the small of my back, and held me close. His thinness was stark. I could feel his muscle and bone as we started dancing to the music in his head. The farm's smell was on his clothes, a sharp, animal musk. *One, two, one, two*: a swaying, slow, nothing dance. As he moved my body around the yellow-walled room with all its spinning finery, I felt my throat constricting.

Once I had seen a documentary about men who have relationships with inflatable dolls. The camera crew arrive at a house, and show, through a bedroom door, an unblinking, pore-less, woman-sized doll lying in bed, a sheet just covering its plastic breasts. 'We've had a pretty active morning,' the doll owner swaggers. He's playing at being post-coital: they've apparently just been surprised in the act of love, and chivalrously he closes the door on the doll's open-mouthed leer. Later, this man carefully dresses this doll in a demure blouse and skirt, and then poses it on a deckchair at the top of a cliff to admire him hang-gliding. At one point, the film cuts to a doll maker, or a doll repairer, his house full of plastic body parts with which he fixes the dolls' various holes. Despite his work, the man seems normal enough, bemused by his obsessive clients, until he turns to the camera, making a confession. Once he'd been fixing an incredibly lifelike doll. This doll kept giving him the eye. It wanted it badly, and eventually he'd broken, and taken *her*.

As Alexander shifted me from side to side I felt like that doll. He pressed my head against his chest, and glancing down I watched his thick woollen socks against the Persian carpet, bunching up around his toes. *One, two, one, two* – how vulnerable people are when they dance badly. He was leading from his groin. Lost in some reverie, he moved to his song, while I was waiting, swaying and waiting. I could hear him breathing, smell his breath; his whiskers brushed my skin as he bent down to kiss my forehead, his warm hand pressing harder on the small of my back.

When he kissed my forehead again, he glanced sideways.

I realised Alexander had us dancing in front of the room's tall gilt mirror. Everything caught within its frame was too splendid; all the antiques seemed inlaid with exotic woods and wreathes of brass, their lines curving, swirling, as if the very purpose was to disorientate. And he was watching us in the treasure's midst, posing us. As he turned me, I saw a glaze of pleasure cross his face; here was a child given something he'd felt beyond his reach.

It had hardened, not softened him and I recalled suddenly the feeling of being pinned underneath his body, so I couldn't move and couldn't breathe. It had happened once, perhaps twice, and when finally he'd released me, I rolled to the side, hungry for air, as he lay watching. Now he swung me around so I was facing the mirror, looking like a creature about to be swallowed.

I broke away.

Alexander ran his fingers through his hair, glancing up from downcast eyes. 'I've shocked you.'

My voice barely worked. 'A little.'

'I'm surprised you are surprised. You must have known how I felt?'

I half nodded – it was all I could manage. *Do I play along with this?* I wondered. *Is that why I'm here?*

'Liese, are you feeling like you're floating?' he whispered.

'In a way.'

'I feel so light.' Still partly in his dance, he was completely unguarded. 'So relieved, I suppose . . .'

'Could I please have a drink?'

'. . . it's like a dream.' He glanced at me again and to my relief there was a flicker of humour. 'Oh, of course, the champagne.'

Alexander left the room and I sat down on the couch, checking first for its edge. This must be some fetish he has – *à la* hookers dressed as schoolgirls, I reasoned. The engagement ring was just on loan while he played out his bridal fantasy; *that* was why he was paying me so much.

For those wanting to extend the Girlfriend Experience presumably one could upgrade to the Fiancée Experience, and feel giddy with the promise of a new life without the inconvenience of an actual marriage. Maybe he thought it was safe to indulge in this with me because soon I'd be leaving the country.

He returned with two long-stemmed glasses and the bottle of Australian *méthode champenoise* from our picnic; there was the slightest strut to his walk.

'This is a nice drop, very smooth.' Peeling the foil from the cork, opening it, he grinned. 'Let's drink to your happiness.'

Not knowing how far to take the act, I acted poorly. 'No, to *our* happiness.' I drank too quickly.

'It's good.' He rocked slightly on the balls of his feet, staring into his glass with a sly look of pride. 'I wanted this to be perfect. All of it.'

Holding out my glass for a refill, I wondered, Will I need to keep this up for another two whole days?

'I've thought of how it would happen many times.'

Trying to smile: 'Have you really?'

'Do you know when I fell for you?' He raised his eyebrows. 'It was the first time we met and you were trying to find the right door key. I could see into your handbag and there was a copy of Ovid's *Metamorphoses*.' He was chuckling, remembering. 'And that's when I had an inkling you were for me. She must be very smart, I thought. She must read all the time. That book's one people always refer to, don't they?'

Alexander straightened. 'With the demands of the farm, and, of course, the children, it will be difficult to get away to Melbourne as often as we might want.' He glanced at me, subtly checking his words' effect. 'So I'm pleased you like books. There's also the piano,' indicating the upright in the corner. 'I've been thinking, perhaps I could get you lessons . . . No, really! You think I'm joking, but piano music's very soothing.' He nodded, for a moment suitably bashful. 'You could play to the baby while he is, you know, inside you. And then, when he's older, he can learn himself.'

Alexander grinned again, acknowledging his own indulgence. He put his hand to his heart. 'I will solemnly promise from the outset to do most of the cooking, because you'll have your hands full, Liese.' He focused on the middle distance. 'I want my kids raised very differently to the way I was. My parents were nineteenth-century, essentially. Brought up themselves by nannies, and born to people raised the same way. My mother probably had postnatal depression, although the doctors and hospitals didn't know what it was then, and God knows, my father gave her no support.'

He took a box of matches from behind a vase on the mantelpiece, and returning to bended knee, adjusted the kindling in the grate. 'My father preferred it when Mum *was* locked up. No, neither of them was able to show love. I've forgiven my parents for that – one has to – but my children will have it from me. None of this just getting some teenager to watch over the kids while slavishly keeping up appearances.' Alexander shook his head, turning back to me. 'Do you know what I mean?'

I coughed. 'You seem to have put a lot of thought into this.'

'Other people's opinions don't matter to me.'

Including, I noticed, mine on marriage or procreation. Sitting on the couch, I watched him light the fire, taking in his every movement, waiting for some slip to reveal he was only playing a role.

'Inevitably the au pairs were miserable out here anyway. These girls would come, foreigners more often than not – don't ask me how my mother found them – and after a month, they'd try to leave any way they could. Once, during shearing season, one lass ran off with a shearer in the middle of the night – at least, we assumed that's what happened,' he recalled, grinning. 'Poor me! Aged five, I'd fall for some nineteen-year-old who'd very soon disappear . . . Give me the old days: when servants escaped they were hunted down and brought back.'

'Like slaves,' I said softly.

He turned around again. 'Exactly like slaves.'

We stared at each other.

He picked up a poker, playing with his fire. 'I don't think we should wait too long before trying to conceive. We won't be the youngest parents, but that means there are certain advantages we'll bring to the job. Wisdom, a degree of patience. As for how many, it's up to you, largely.' He turned again. 'You're thirty-three? Thirty-four?'

Slowly, I nodded. 'We could have at least half a dozen babies, potentially . . .' I was acting along to test if this *was* still an act.

'If you can, wonderful.'

'. . . and definitely no nannies. I'd prefer to do all of it without any help.'

Standing, brushing off his trousers, he looked pleased, immune now to irony.

'It will just be you and me and the children alone in this house . . .' My voice trailed off. By some trick of perspective the mirror had shrunk us, turning the whole room into a diorama; the woman behind the glass playing me sat tense on the couch, hands clenched in her lap, as the man, uncoiling with his plans, set himself free.

Glancing into the mirror, Alexander met my gaze. 'You don't look happy.' His voice was sharp.

Should I earn my fee and play along, I wondered, or end this before it goes any further?

'There's no need to be frightened.' He said this like it was a stage direction.

'Everything's happened so fast, that's all.'

Reaching down, Alexander touched my neck, stroked it. 'Tell me, Liese, what is it?'

'Nothing.'

'Is someone holding something over you?'

'What sort of thing?'

'Perhaps compromising information?' His stubbled face was leaning right over mine, and with his fingers on my throat it felt as though he were taking my pulse. The way he touched me now was careful. He was making clear he respected – *what* was it, my personal space? my honour? Sex had been our breathing line and without it we were down too deep and dangerous. 'Perhaps,' his voice was soft, coaxing, 'perhaps you owe people money?'

Any reflex to laugh had gone. 'Only Mr Visa.'

He did not seem to hear me. 'I could help you pay them off.' Oblivious to the fact he had been, he picked up his glass and sat next to me, leaning back into the sofa's cushions. 'Truly, just tell me the amount. How bad can it be, Liese? I'll write a cheque, and all this will be over.

'Look, I don't want to spoil this by turning to business, but in my letter inviting you here, I promised a percentage of your fee would be paid into your account at the end of the weekend.

Despite our engagement I will stay true to my word.' Clearing his throat, he almost looked shy. 'If it's not presumptuous of me, I'd like you to think of this as your dowry.'

'My *dowry*?'

'Exactly. I don't want you to worry about money, about . . .' he hesitated, 'the discrepancies between our financial situations. So I propose paying you an allowance.' He reached for the champagne bottle to refill both our glasses. 'As long as everything is progressing in a satisfactory manner.'

The fire was stirring my memory of heat.

'What do you mean by satisfactory?'

Alexander's face twisted slightly. 'I think it's pretty clear.'

'Yes?'

'I would expect – no,' he caught himself, nodding, 'no, I would *appreciate* your continuing to provide the current services, plus maintaining the household, and supervising the care of our children.'

'I see.'

'Good.' He stood, wiping his palms on his trousers.

'So marriage is an arrangement where you can have sex with the babysitter?'

Exhaling: 'Potentially, it can be a lot more than that.'

'Alexander,' I said carefully – my claim to any higher ground was average at best – 'I would never be happy in a marriage that's just a glorified business deal.'

'I've told you, I love you,' he flared, exasperated. 'What more do you want?'

'You don't even know me!'

He'd moved to a bureau on the other side of the room. 'I do, and what I don't know I will learn. We'll learn together.' He opened one drawer after the other, searching for something. 'I realise you've seen the world, that you've met all kinds of . . . people, which for your sake and mine I won't dwell on here. But despite that, despite the *situations*,' his expression again contorted, 'in which you've found yourself, you've retained a certain self-possession, even an innocence that I admire.'

Slamming closed the last drawer, irritated, he turned further from me, his hand now shielding his face. 'Besides,' his back gave the slightest quiver, 'I know more about you than you think. More, quite frankly, than I really want to know.'

From outside there came the rhythmic night shift of frogs.

'Are you crying?' I asked eventually.

Alexander wiped at his cheek, trying to smile. 'Sometimes I think of what you've had to deal with.'

His tears shocked me. 'I'm sorry?'

'I lie awake and think of them with their hands all over you, making you do whatever it is they want . . . I mean, I'm only human – of course I get jealous. I love you and so it follows I'm jealous, all right?' Grimacing, he shut his bloodshot eyes and made a low, slow moan. 'I try not to picture it, but sometimes I can't stop. I can't get the images of you with them out of my mind. Over and over I see all the things they made you do . . .'

'Excuse me, I need a glass of water.' Standing, I walked out of the room.

I could not do this. I just could not. Even if this was a fetish, it had become too strange, too head-fucking. Other than physically,

I realised I didn't know this man well, but I thought I knew him well enough to be sure he wasn't crazy.

Clearly I'd made a terrible error telling my one client I would be leaving the country. I'd hoped by giving fair warning I was showing him the sort of courtesy he would have shown me. Besides, I could not have him visiting my uncle's office, asking for another hooker. Had I considered cancelling this weekend beforehand? Not really. Stuck as I was on the payoff, I'd prepared for the trip with great concentration. I'd planned my wardrobe from the underwear out, sitting at my cubicle, pen poised unused in the air, anticipating some personalised *Belle de Jour*.

Alexander was now following me through the cold warren of the house. The lights were turned off, and the smell in certain dark corners seemed to be of damp that had grown into rot.

'Liese, you don't have to do those things any more,' he called, mimicking concern, 'none of them!'

'I'll do whatever I want!' I snapped, feeling around on the kitchen wall for a light switch, patting the bluestone harder and harder. If I chose to start screwing hundreds of strangers and charging for it, I damn well would. 'Have you ever heard of such a thing as free will?'

He reached over me to flick the switch. 'Not in these cases.'

At the sink I filled a glass with water.

'And I've read a fair bit of literature about women in your situation.'

'Really? Because you're the one who had to pay for it – shouldn't I be crying for you?' I banged down the glass without drinking. 'I want to go home.'

'Well, I can't drive you tonight. Not after the champagne.'

I stared at him. 'Tomorrow I'd like you to take me to a railway station.'

He nodded solemnly, as though this would be possible, then opened the fridge door. 'How peckish are you?'

After seeing the sweet, depressed faces of the animals in the fields, I couldn't eat more meat. 'The best thing for me right now is probably sleep, then in the morning I want to go.'

'But I was planning to cook for you.'

'I don't feel like eating.'

'*Okay.*' He raised both eyebrows. 'Are you at least prepared to sit with me while I have my dinner?'

I didn't answer but neither did I leave. Methodically he took ingredients out of the fridge, cracking eggs into a bowl, beating them; he grated cheese, he poured in milk. The dim light made everything grained as though my sight had suddenly deteriorated. I sat at the table, scanning the room as if the assortment of inherited crockery would give some clue to his sanity – and to whether he actually lived in this house alone. Not one object seemed to have been chosen by him. I kept half expecting one of his parents to return and tell Alexander off for playing with his mother's jewellery.

Raising my hands to my head, my throbbing head, I caught the reflection of the ring's diamond across the wall.

Alexander was warming a skillet. 'I carried that ring around with me everywhere, worried sick you might leave the country. I'd have done anything to keep you here. It was all I could think about, and I wanted this day to be perfect.' He poured his mixture onto the hot iron. 'It's naïve of me, because nothing's ever how you picture it, is it?'

I almost felt sorry for him. 'It's still been a nice day, Alexander.'

When his omelette was ready he took a plate and served himself. Sitting down opposite me he began to eat in silence.

The scent of the food was headier than I'd expected. I tried not to feel hunger.

'We could at least talk about something,' he said peevishly.

'All right, what?'

'Politics, history . . . just, you know, conversation?'

'What happened to your parents?' I'd noticed nothing specific to them anywhere in the house, their photographs weren't alongside those of the ancestors.

He paused. 'A car accident.'

'How did it happen?'

'It was New Year's Eve, 1986. A dark road. Probably both drunk.'

'That must have been very difficult. Do you have siblings?'

'An older sister.'

'Are you close?'

'Not really.' He stood, stretching to his full height, and took his plate to the sink; an opacity had set around him. 'I don't want you to hold the things I've told you about my mother's illness against her, she was a wonderful person and our engagement would have meant the world to her. Despite being born into great privilege – at one time her family pretty much owned half the district – she was not a snob,' Alexander assured me.

He ran the taps and started washing the plate and mixing bowl, using no-name detergent and an old wire brush. 'She'd want me to be happy and she'd have been delighted, despite our different backgrounds, that the two of us have found each other – really delighted.' He started on the skillet, and with his sleeves rolled up I could see the stark line of his tan. When his shirt was off he was just as pale below his collar.

'Even when Mum was in the depths of misery, she wanted joy for others.'

Near me, balancing on the shelves of the cupboard, was his calendar with June's bull; I noticed it was a gift from *The Artificial Insemination Specialists*.

'I think she'd want me to have a family – no, no, I know that.'

It was perverse, but studying the picture I suddenly remembered this man's semen running down the inside of my thighs – I had to get upstairs and hide my contraceptive pills. There were another ten days left on the foil, and what if he tried to flush them away? Was Alexander's showing me the farm, his kingdom, the warm-up for an Old Testament-type story about a man who needs to beget a workforce of sons?

'Liese.' He knew I'd drifted off. 'As I said, I've done my homework about your trade, and I know to you I must have sometimes seemed just as bad as the rest of the johns. You must have felt, Oh, here comes another one trying to exploit me.'

I stared at him. 'But I *chose* this.'

He placed the skillet on the drying rack, his expression one of simple bewilderment. 'You might tell yourself that to maintain some self-respect, but how could you? How could you choose to be an object that's bought and sold? A slave might to some extent give consent, but that's because she doesn't realise she has an alternative. She doesn't *have* to allow strangers to grunt away on top of her.'

Alexander's logic froze me.

'I mean, I imagine it's very humiliating to admit that you're a victim. And hard for someone like you to face the facts of your . . .' he opted for frankness, 'your abuse. Especially if it's been long-term. And so to hold onto any pride you prop yourself up with nonsense words like "choice" and "agency".'

Behind him the window frames made neat squares out of darkness.

'How will *you* stop abusing me?' I asked quietly.

'I'll marry you,' he answered. 'As soon as possible.'

Lying in the narrow bed I felt like I'd been buried. The house was wheezing, making strangely human noises. The glass panes of the window rattled, then there was silence.

No one knows where I am.

Pictures from the tiny towns we'd skirted kept running through my head: a shop with the windows boarded over, a grey stone church deserted on a hill, and then the land flattening to paddocks of sheep and cattle until the dense bush of the national park.

He thinks he can do what he likes with me.

I found the switch on the bedside lamp – a dull glow spread under its shade. My suitcase was waiting slumped by the door.

Carefully, lest the mattress springs gave me away, I folded back the heavy blankets and climbed out of the bed. I was shivering, wearing a ridiculous lace slip I'd ordered on the internet when I was supposed to be working. I picked up my case, and laying it on the rosebud bedspread began quietly to pack my clothes.

This was absurd! Presumably Alexander wanted to purify his desire, not eradicate it. But the whole point of marriage was to cancel out the erotic. It was essentially a contract between two people so as *not* to have to sleep together. Within a few years, I knew – from my recent scouting of other people's houses – it was finger-paintings on the fridge, a StairMaster exercise machine facing the television. In the master bedroom, *Keeping Families Strong* on one bedside table, and on the other a history of aviation – fight and flight. I had heard of an agreement a French woman signed with her husband, forcing an annulment as soon as he ceased to desire her, but people usually tied the knot so they could *get over* desire, so they weren't driven mad by it, and could eventually cease copulating altogether.

I thought of my own mother and father – I had to get them both a present before I left the country. There would be something for them at the airport. Kangaroo salt-and-pepper shakers, T-shirts embossed with koalas. Taking this suitcase and the cash in the envelope, I could just go straight there and buy a ticket to Shanghai, and fly to my real future, my bright, real future.

It must have been mid-morning back in England: my parents would be at home running their own sheltered workshop, my mother writing a list of tasks for my father to keep him out of her sight. He would tidy his tiny garden, then fix some small broken thing out in the shed, glue a handle back onto a milk jug they'd been given as a wedding present – trying to stay out of her way.

My mother had cautioned my younger sister and me at length on the shortcomings of men, but she still wanted us each to find one. When all her friends' daughters started donning their white dresses and marching, one after the other, down the aisle, she quietly sneered at the farce of it all – the smug bride, holding tight to her prize-winner, bovine in his rented morning suit; the bridesmaids, weepy, self-important, envious, the fattest one inevitably chosen to read out the sonnet. But as each village burgher's daughter was married off – and the same baby toy, now bought in bulk, was sent the following year – my mother made it clear she felt I was crossing some line into freakdom.

Back at home people paired off as if they had prior warning of a flood. So one benefit of leaving the country had been not hearing her sigh each time she reported another girl's engagement (just the word sounding clammy, claustrophobic: a room no one could enter, a number no one could call). An engagement was the beginning of one long silent fight that, judging from my parents' example, could go on for decades.

When my sister became engaged (the ring like a performance indicator: her life was tracking correctly) my mother and I accompanied her to a bridal superstore, to rows and rows of shining, ruched gowns that she hoarded in her changing room. Emerging in them one by one, she stood in the communal fitting area, amongst the other dozen women in white dresses who each stared stunned into the mirrors, multiplying further.

I watched on, carrying a white wicker shopping basket which

held an ivory satin ring cushion trimmed with lace and ribbons (£24.99), and the blue lace garter (£14.35), and the memorial pen set, with dangling heart charms, for the registry signing (£29.50). To decorate the tables, there were mini-champagne-bottle bubble-blowers (£0.69 each), gold heart-sparklers (£0.99 a stick), wedding trivia sets – *What was the first movie [insert bride's name] and [insert groom's] saw together?* (£9.95), and, as a party favour for the ladies, 'Happily Ever After' Cinderella Carriage candles (£1.95 each), and for the men 'Love is Blooming' seed packets (£1.25 a pop).

I had not been asked to be a bridesmaid. Did I expect to be? I suppose so. But my sister, who still lived in Norwich, had stayed very close to her group of schoolfriends, who'd all look pretty in the same way for the photographs. I also knew she thought I wasn't taking her big day seriously enough; in fact I was taking it as seriously as my hurt allowed.

The day before the wedding my father glued little white satin rosebuds onto the place cards, then, as the artistic one, I wrote the guests' names in calligraphy copied from a book. When I suggested the cards would be more elegant without the roses, my sister called me a snob.

That night, the four of us – my parents and sister and me – sat in the lounge room on the couch and its matching recliners, my mother's framed posters of Renoir's bosomy market girls on the walls around us, all of us eating off the plates we'd always eaten off, my parents' wedding china, holding a kind of vigil. We were trying to be jolly but each one of us resented the other three for making us who we were. I knew my sister actually believed that by marrying she would stage an escape, and she retreated early to the room which had once been hers, hoping to get this night over with.

The reception was in a Jacobean stately home, ten miles away. Guests drank champagne in a room with a dusty velvet rope round the walls, while outside the bridal party were documented in the parterre gardens, then next to an ornamental lake, then playing croquet, my sister with satin wedding horseshoes around her wrist like some smith of kitsch; Lord and Lady Poor-Now watching from their private wing, chortling.

In the family portrait I am wearing a charcoal Helmut Lang dress, which, my sister claimed, made me resemble a jagged raincloud. My mother's face is streaked with tears, and my father blushes from high feeling. My brother-in-law – in a lavender bow tie to match the bridesmaids' dresses – has a wide fixed grin; his new wife's determined happiness is creating a slipstream meant to pull everyone along after her.

The next day, I took the train back to London feeling I'd been marked by a bad fairy. I thought of the Larkin poem we'd studied at school.

> . . . *the wedding-days*
> *Were coming to an end. All down the line*
> *Fresh couples climbed aboard: the rest stood round;*
> *The last confetti and advice were thrown . . .*

The crabby poet had once taken an afternoon train on Whit Sunday, an auspicious day to marry, and at each station more newlyweds alighted, travelling to their London honeymoons, giving him a momentary sense of hope and renewal. But as I returned from my sister's wedding – her 'happy funeral', as Larkin put it – the train rocketing through the gauze light, the view was so blurred and grey it seemed the sky was permanently set to dusk, and I felt the opposite: unhopeful, un-renewed.

Soon after arriving in Liverpool Street I needed to go shopping. It was always like this: the purchase acting as a kind of bloodletting. If I didn't do it, I'd feel ill; ill or non-existent. Buying an overpriced handbag promised to restore me to life – the life I wanted. The salesgirl now my true judge as she took the credit card without meeting my eye, possessing a psychic sense it could be declined, recognising too, somehow, that I had just been back at home helping glue satin rosebuds onto name cards. Knowing all about me in this place meant to hide everything, a customer trap hewn of marble and glass and nothingness.

In the seconds waiting for the transaction to go through I was conscious I could barely afford my glorified Notting Hill bedsit, and that a spate of my possessions had recently got together and agreed to break down, and that this purchase would trigger a period of abstemiousness that would end with me again spending money as if I actually had it – how much it cost not to seem poor! But instead I feigned nonchalance, waiting in the shimmering air until the card was miraculously approved – and as the salesgirl passed over the handbag wrapped in freshest tissue paper, and I walked out into the street, for a moment the world had a special lustre.

Now, in this pink bedroom, I'd stuffed all my clothes into the suitcase. The last thing to pack was the envelope of money.

I took it out from the drawer and again checked the contents – Australian currency in all its psychedelic colours, the pine-green hundreds like a Nordic acid trip. I decided to put it in the case's concealed pocket. I closed the lid, zipping the whole thing up. I grabbed the handle and swung it off the bed. It was heavier than I expected. And my grip was wrong. And the case tipped – it tipped and thudded to the floor.

The whole house tensed.

I closed my eyes, waiting.

Do other people have a room in their heads? Enter it and close the door. Anything can happen and no one will see you. Act as you like and then act it again; slow the scene down or speed it up until each second starts to glow, electrified . . .

The problem being that I had started acting outside the room as I did inside. 'Live the Dream!' 'Lifestyle Opportunity' read every real-estate flier and billboard of every house we entered – and I'd had the idea that I could just flip over into the world of my subconscious and let it rule. Basically, I would make sex pay.

Now I heard Alexander coming up the stairs. I waited, untangling his sounds from those of the house. His footfall heavy, deliberate; last night's game of silence was over. He approached the door of my room, then hesitated.

Turning off the bedside lamp, I grabbed the ring box.

A knock on the door. 'Liese, is your head feeling better now?'

Stretched out on top of the stiff bedclothes, I called back in a voice too cheerful, 'Fine, thank you.'

A slither of light as Alexander opened the door. 'I heard noise.'

'No.' I tried to breathe regularly, even this pillow smelled sour. 'I was just lying here.'

I could not see his face. But on the floor between us my suitcase was visible, exploded with clothes.

When eventually he spoke, he sounded puzzled. 'We have a big day tomorrow.'

'I'll get some rest.'

There was another long pause. 'You've made me very happy tonight. I want to make you just as happy.'

Was there something else he was debating whether to say?

Moving to close the door he murmured, 'Goodnight again.'

'Goodnight.'

I lay still – this darkness had thickness to it, it had weight. My fingers clutched the box.

Alexander was standing on the other side of the door. I just knew he was. He was standing there while I kept my breathing shallow, the air barely travelling to my lungs. Both of us seemed to be waiting for the other to make a move.

He walked away from the door, but not before I heard a scraping. A scratching of metal like a key was turning in the lock.

Cold surged through me – I had invited him into my most private room. Once there, he'd taken my fantasy and bent it out of shape. Bent it until, by the thinnest, finest chance, I found I'd slid somewhere dank, unknown. I was inside the room in *his* head and he had locked the door.

II

The next morning the handle turned easily. I found myself in the hallway surrounded by closed doors, all of them painted the colour of sour milk. Had my door been locked in the first place?

Downstairs in the kitchen, Alexander was leaning forward at the table, closely reading a newspaper: a model of angular rectitude on the day of rest. Even unshaven as he was, his features appeared neat and regular. Here was the most ordinary of men. The table before him seemed ordinary too: jam in a willow-pattern bowl, fresh butter on its dish, triangles of toast in their silver holder. And propped beside my bread plate, an envelope. It looked like one of those I'd seen in his desk drawer the day before.

Mr Alexander Colquhoun
'Warrowill'
Marshdale
Victoria

He folded the newspaper crisply, giving a mild, tight smile. 'How did you sleep?'

'Fine,' I lied.

'The dogs didn't wake you?'

'No.' Although I'd heard them answering birdcall as I watched the walls turn blue then gold then back to pink as eventually the sun rose.

'I don't know what you like for breakfast,' Alexander noted. 'Generally I have toast and tea.'

'Perfect.' I tried to stay upbeat, daylight making this situation appear manageable.

He gestured I should help myself, and without ceremony resumed his position with the newspaper.

I took a slice of toast and ate quietly. If he'd noticed I wasn't wearing the engagement ring he did not mention it. No reference was made to his proposal, to the plans for our bright future. In fact, Alexander seemed almost uninterested in me. He turned the pages slowly, as though reading every paragraph, every word in every line.

I waited.

I'd heard of men who liked to take hookers in white dresses, feeling the crisp rustling tulle, the smooth satin, while pretending the women were debutantes or brides. This must have been the same style of thing. He had some fetish, some script he wanted to role-play, but I'd evidently been something of a disappointment, and now it was over. I hadn't wept with him about the strangers who'd abused my body, nor prostrated myself in gratitude at his saving me from the abuse. That, I guessed, was why I was receiving this silent treatment. Alexander may have been sulking but I hoped he might also be relieved when he took me to the railway station; he could simply put the ring back in a drawer and go about his business. I wondered why I had lain in bed rigid with fear.

The kitchen was chilled, and perfectly still. Its walls had been painted long ago – everything white was now grey. Out the window were the bare trees of the orchard.

'What fruit do you grow?' I asked to stop the silence.

'Apples, quince, plums . . .' He did not look up.

'When did the gardener, all the gardeners, leave?'

'The sixties.'

I waited for a moment. 'What happened then?'

'Not one thing. Overheads, markets, exchange rates, exhausted soil – you name it. My father's bloody incompetence.'

'You didn't like him much, did you?'

He looked up from the paper. 'It doesn't matter whether one "likes" one's parents. It's juvenile to expect one should.'

He kept reading, and as I waited I began to sense *his* strange impatience. I had a sudden feeling he'd been in the kitchen with this scene set, expecting each element – myself included – to conform to the script in his head: *Sitting at the table having breakfast.*

'Perhaps you'd like the arts pages?'

'No, I'm fine – oh, thank you.' I took them from his outstretched hand, and I saw today's date. 'Do you have this delivered?'

'Out here? No. I picked it up in town.'

'So you've driven in? Already?'

'You were quite safe here.'

Safe? Because he'd locked the door of my room? 'I would've liked to come. How long does the drive take?'

'Half an hour each way.' He leaned back. 'So, will I read you the Odd Spot?' Affability: I felt him straining towards it. 'That's the little whimsical piece on the front page.'

'I know.'

'All right, so: "A British Columbia woman called police after mistaking her neighbour's noisy toilet efforts for a violent disturbance. The woman heard yelling and shouting and believed that . . ."'

I wondered whether I could catch a bus from this town back to Melbourne, if it would be easier than the train.

Alexander did his closed-mouth chuckle. 'Sorry, did that offend you?'

I looked up, realising I had been meant to join him. 'Not at all.'

'You didn't find it amusing?'

'No, it's amusing.' A featherless dead goose was lying on a tray near the sink. 'But . . . I, I'm not good with jokes.'

'It wasn't a joke.'

I shrugged, blocking any picture of the bird's end. Until this weekend, I must have seemed permanently on heat. *But this is what I'm really like*, I wanted to say, *uptight, dull.*

Alexander regarded me closely. 'Humour isn't everything, Liese, but I think it's important to be able to laugh at the world.'

Usually I could. Usually I could do nothing but laugh.

He followed my gaze to the bird. 'Well,' he flexed his fingers, 'I've stocked up on supplies, and it's a perfect day to cook a feast.'

Standing, coming behind me, he carefully placed a hand on my head.

'Unfortunately I have to go back to Melbourne this afternoon.'

'But you're staying until tomorrow.'

Had he forgotten last night, my telling him I was leaving? I could not see his face, whether he was testing me. 'It turns out I've got work. Real-estate work,' I added stupidly. 'An emergency has just come up at the office.'

'How did you find out?' His fingers spread, pressing into my scalp.

'My uncle . . . his assistant's been sick . . .'

'I wouldn't have thought your phone would have reception here.'

When I had no answer, Alexander said, 'Wear your hair down like this, it suits you.' He moved from behind me, keeping his face neutral. His little victory hung in the air between us as he took an apron from a hook on the back of the door and tied it around himself. He rolled up his sleeves.

The goose's torso was a strange, amputated thing, the stumps of its feet and wings and head still bloodied.

'Now,' he chuckled again, 'have you ever gutted such a damned big bird?'

I shook my head at my own foolishness.

'Neither have I, but I promised I would cook for you.'

'Don't trouble yourself.'

'But I want to. Liese, this is what normal couples do.' He spoke almost sweetly, although as if giving instructions. 'One person has interests and the other tries to be interested in those interests. The two of them then find things to do in common.'

He was so much taller than me even without shoes, and sliding over the red linoleum in his thick woollen socks, slouching just slightly, he took a book down from a shelf: *Home Butchery & Meat Preservation*. His pelvis tilted against the kitchen bench, he straightened the book's spine on the formica. He licked his index finger and flipped through the pages. Each move he made reminded me of sex with him. And now the memories weren't so pleasing.

Perching one foot against his ankle, he absent-mindedly scratched at his shin. His socks had a crest on them – rows of tiny royal lions and stars. Were they school socks? I felt repulsion. I felt it even for his toes that I'd once had inside my mouth. It was horrible that I had ever desired him.

The book was open to a diagram of a bird in X-ray.

Picking up a steel, he casually sharpened his knife. 'When I was a child Warrowill did all its own butchering, but my father thought it too time-consuming. A steer can take two men the best part of a day. He stopped it, although he wasn't often around to check. The men took cows that couldn't get in calf and butchered them on their days off.'

Tentatively Alexander put his hand on the goose and made the first incision, a long deep cut, his face locking in a frown as his wrist then went into the hole, this nightmare creature like his puppet.

He wanted me to be scared and I resented it. 'Now butchery's terribly fashionable, of course,' I said coolly.

'Is that right?'

'Yes.'

The organic café near my studio in Notting Hill advertised classes in venison butchery. The *beau monde* couldn't get enough of evisceration – it made them feel their lives weren't just about accounting.'

'Can you cook?' he asked after a silence.

I grimaced. His hand – the one that had just stroked my hair – was now a raspberry colour, a deep slime-pink. 'Not really. It's not my thing.'

'No, the English, I forget . . .'

Outside the dogs barked as though they could sense his work.

'You should see your expression – it's a cartoon of disapproval,' Alexander said, tugging at something dense and entwined. One or two grabs and the intestines emerged, wrapped around other oozing, complicated, vermilion parts. He threw the tangle into a yellow bucket, picking out the heart and liver and putting them to one side. 'But perhaps you will think of learning? Learning to cook?'

Now he began hacking at the carcass, at the windpipe perhaps. I can't believe he's holding an actual cleaver, I was thinking. How melodramatic, how desperate, and yet my hand went to my mouth: the sight, the smell, were overwhelming.

'Liese, sometimes I can't get away from the farm until late,' Alexander's face was also strained, 'and I'd like it if you knew how to prepare something other than pasta.'

Standing now, I leaned against the table. 'No one at home is much of a cook,' I admitted cautiously. I'd never told him about my family, sensing this wasn't what he wished to hear. 'Mum does okay, but Dad can't even open a can of soup.'

Alexander scowled with surprise. 'Mum and Dad?'

'Yes.'

'I assumed you'd lost contact with them, or that they were both —' He stopped himself, using his sleeve to move a curl from his eyes. 'What do these parents of yours do?'

'Before retirement, an engineer and a . . . homemaker.'

'A homemaker?' He put down the cleaver, assessing my candour. 'You mean a housewife?' He repeated the word, trying to convince himself. 'And they don't know about your . . . *profession*?'

My packed suitcase was waiting upstairs. I'd put it back together before coming down to breakfast. There was nothing I'd left in the bathroom. I could just pick up the case and leave.

'What is your father's name?'

I hesitated. 'It's Robert.'

'*Robert* – and his surname?'

'Campbell.'

'All right then,' he almost rolled his eyes, 'I suppose I should call Mr Campbell and ask him officially for your hand in marriage.' This complication annoyed him. 'And may I ask if Liese is your actual name?'

I nodded.

'So, Robert Campbell will presumably know who I'm talking about?' Alexander went to the sink and began washing his hands, then his wrists, now also covered in the bird's liquids. He turned off the tap, the pipes creaking, and started rifling impatiently through a drawer, pulling out a pad and a thin silver pencil. 'Why don't you write down the number for me?'

'Of course.' I went over and took the pencil, pivoting my body so he would not see my hands tremble. If I could get to the telephone I would call for a taxi. This situation was now beyond my realm of expertise: perhaps I could handle this man, but no longer did I wish to try. 'Do you think I could quickly ring my parents and let them know you'll be in touch?'

He didn't answer.

'I'll reverse the charges,' I said, keeping my voice casual. 'The thing is, I haven't yet mentioned that we've been seeing each other.'

'I'm not surprised.'

Giggling weakly: 'But I should think they'll be thrilled . . . Alexander, where is the phone?'

Picking up his knife again, he started cutting at something in the bird's open cavity. 'It's the middle of the night over there.'

'My parents won't mind!' That was the irony: even if I *were* trapped miles from anywhere with a sociopath, my mother would be delighted I was finally engaged.

'It's not the sort of first impression I want to make. I'll call tonight — Fuck!'

'What is it?'

'I haven't unhooked the gallbladder properly, and now there's bile on the bird's meat.' He seemed to feel this was my fault. Agitated, glancing around, he grabbed a cloth, then another knife, and tried to wipe and cut away the problem. 'Liese, before you start calling Robert and . . . ?'

'Sue.'

'Robert and Sue,' he nodded, 'with your happy news, can I ask you why you chose this career?'

'Please don't start that again.'

His neck was strained with irritation. 'Well, if you're not actually a whore then I want my money back.'

There was no point trying to convince him that this was a case of mistaken identity, because surely Alexander knew the precise nature of the mistake.

'I've told you I'm prepared to put your past behind us,' he went on, 'but I'm just trying to understand, okay? I'm just trying to understand because you seem very normal, very sensible. Why did you get into prostitution so young? You were only a teenager, still in school.'

'I've never told you that.'

'You didn't need to.' Pursing his mouth, his expression turned sceptical. 'Your father, Robert, was he a drunk, or violent?'

I shook my head, hating that he now knew my father's name.

'I mean, did he, did he *do* something to you?'

'No!' I found myself shouting.

Alexander held out a flattened palm. 'Don't get so defensive.'

He went back to studying his book, and through my rage came a sudden clear thought: This man is punishing me for not loving him. Our relationship was meant to be devoid of love. That was its whole point. Yet part of him despised me for being in it for the money. Did it always come down to this? The client deciding: You are only a whore, how dare you not genuinely want exactly what I want. Do as I say – love me as I desire, of your own free will. Not that I believed Alexander actually loved me. He didn't even know me. My body was a stand-in for whoever really hadn't returned his devotion.

This room's stink kept edging closer.

'Did anyone try to hit you? Were they dangerous?'

I could hear my heart beating, my blood. 'No, never.'

'Was it something you allowed, if they asked?'

'I'm afraid not, Alexander.'

'That's fortunate,' he said quickly. 'You are very lucky, because you hear about it all the time: some adventure's gone awry and a young girl ends face down in a faraway ditch.' He presented the image without emotion, looking up from his work to gauge the effect. 'I imagine the most frightening thing would be to end up with someone not right in the head. For all you knew at first, *I* could have been a psycho.'

Alexander continued cutting at the bird, but I could tell there was more, that he was blocking some longer speech – and I waited. Nausea swirled around us in the particles of air; I kept waiting. It was so fine, this situation, the signals so faint, like turning for no reason to catch something flicker on the periphery of your vision.

'Look, there's no point keeping this from you,' he broke.

'What?'

'I . . . I don't want us to hide things. I want us to always tell each other what we are *really* feeling.'

I felt unease, so sharp it was a gut-ache. 'I agree.'

Alexander looked at me and closed his eyes, tilting back his head to contain the distress. 'Two months ago a letter arrived.'

Taking a dishcloth he wiped his hands, smearing it with pink. He picked up the envelope addressed to him from the centre of the table, and held it in front of me.

'I've thought about burning this. However,' he was making a resolution, 'I *won't* have secrets between us, Liese. I just won't.'

From within the envelope, he unfolded a sheet of white office paper, which he handed to me. Upon it was typed:

Dear Mr Colquhoun,

A few weeks ago, I was driving when I saw you outside a block of flats in the Docklands with someone calling herself Liese Campbell.

The wise man says, 'Beware the unknown woman, she is like a river whose twistings you do not understand.' He means, you will be dragged under by her, as I was. I had dealings with her back in England and was pulled down all the way. At first I took Liese for a sweet young lady who had fallen into a bad habit. I tried to be a true friend, encourage changes to her career path. All week, when I was not with her, I thought of ways to help her, and ways to satisfy her needs.

But Miss Campbell is a deceitful woman (deceiving no one as thoroughly as herself.) By taking payment for her favours she can say, 'Oh, I don't really want it (i.e. to mount <u>thousands</u> of different men). It is just a job.' Yet it is <u>not</u> just a job. Whoring is her way of controlling her own <u>constant, sick</u> desire, pretending to herself she is not a NYMPHOMANIAC.

Only her price tag stops the rutting. She wants

it all the time, but money keeps you, and all the others, at safe distance. Hand her all you have and the one thing she gives back she's really taking. Not one true word or feeling will come from her lips because how can someone who's frozen inside make what passes for a heart feel love? She takes you for a fool – and every time you give her money you confirm it. Behind your back, she is laughing.

Yours,

A Friend

I stared at the page: trying to take in its claims, my brain rebelled. The words would not crawl towards sense, the sentences turn to thoughts. I'd told no one I was meeting Alexander, let alone taking his money, and obviously I'd never done such a thing before. So how, and why, and *who*? On the top corner of the page was a perfect thumbprint of light red blood: the illiterate's signature – and I knew. I knew with a kind of physical certainty that he had sat at the keyboard in his study and slowly picked off these lies. The pious tone was his alone. Alexander had put this letter in an envelope, addressed it, then posted it to himself.

I glanced at him out of the corner of my eye.

'So, it's true,' he said slowly, his voice catching. 'Everything in your reaction tells me it is true.'

I reached for a kitchen chair, needing to conserve my energy for thought.

I could not exist for him except as something to despise, and so he'd invented evidence that made me despicable. This was like feeling a cocoon form – each silk thread another of his fantasies – while I was being wrapped inside.

'You can see,' he said defiantly, 'why I would be upset?'

'Yes. It's confronting.'

'Confronting?' he repeated sarcastically. All the restraint in his body was now gone; limbs uncoiling, he bent and took the letter from my hands, waving it in my face. 'Confronting? Some pervert is sitting around trying to fill my head with this filth, and that's all you have to say? Tell me who wrote it!'

I stared at him. *You wrote it, you did.*

Veins were wiring his neck with fury: 'Tell me. And I will find him. And I will kill him!'

Was I supposed to act scared? I mean, I was. I was very, very scared. In that moment it was clear just how capable he was of losing control. But I didn't know if revealing my fear would make it easier to get away or far more difficult. 'Alexander.' I affected a strict, hard voice. 'We both know this letter is not true.'

'Oh, of course,' he laughed bitterly, tilting his head, 'it's a hoax.'

'The things it claims are impossible. I have no other clients.' I reached out, trying to calm him. 'There's no one else but you.'

'Please don't act as if I'm stupid.'

'You were the only one. Always . . .' These words were so pathetic. 'None of this is true —'

'Don't lie to me!'

All the knives in the kitchen seemed too close to him.

The more I begged, the less sincere I sounded. I had to think like he did, but my imagination had no tread. 'How could this person possibly have found you?'

Fear flashed across his face.

'I don't know.' He sniffed hard. 'I presume somehow we were recognised.'

'But why? Why would he bother writing to you?'

'You tell me.' Alexander's hand went to the cleaver.

My line came automatically: 'He may be someone with emotional problems.'

'Yeah? He'd probably say the same about you.'

'This person needs help.' Trying to regard Alexander with real sensitivity, real caring, I felt like a poor excuse for a method actor. 'He's been . . . wounded somewhere along the way, badly hurt. And perhaps it is time for him to –' in the film, this would stir something deep within him – 'to face the fact that he needs proper care. Do you believe me?'

He jerked up one lean arm, pulling at his hair. 'I don't know what to believe!' The look in his eye was furious. And remorseful. And pleased.

I was now standing in the oversize kitchen, winter sun still showing every stain and flaw. *How do walls go grey like that? Is it grease? Desperation?* Behind him the bird's carcass was laid out, and nearby were carrots, onions, a bowl of green apples. I'd written an art essay once paraphrasing some book I'd found that claimed the vanitas works of the Flemish masters 'contemplated the ephemeral nature of earthly life', 'the futility of pleasure' and 'the certainty of death' – I'd been clueless then about what this meant.

'Is the envelope postmarked?'

'They've been sent from all over the place.'

'You mean there's more than one?'

He hesitated. 'Oh, yes.'

Positioning myself near the doorway, I announced, 'I don't think, under the circumstances, I can rightly hold you to your proposal.'

He shook his head slowly. 'Liese, you don't know me at all, do you?'

I knew then he was mad. I knew no one could talk him out of his delusions, but that I had to talk myself out of the kitchen. 'How could you ever trust me, Alexander?' My hands in the air, I was trying for the kind of self-disgust that's convincing. 'For God's sake, I'm *so far* from your ideal woman. You deserve better than this!'

'My ideal woman is not ideal,' he said plainly, my turn at the theatrical making him matter-of-fact. He was considering his book's diagram again. 'It's your imperfections that attract me.' He looked up with blue eyes so dark they were almost reflective. 'Liese, I want you to go upstairs and put your engagement ring back on.'

I glanced down at my bare hand.

'Perhaps its value is intimidating, but I bought it for you to wear.' Half smiling: 'I know you're frightened. That's okay because this is frightening for me too.' He nodded, hand to his heart; this sensitivity was a new form of sadism. 'I have been a bachelor a long time, but when it's right, you just know. Now,' he cleared his throat, 'no more drama, all right? This should really be the happiest time of your life.'

I began walking to the hallway.

'Darling?'

Turning, I shivered: he had never used such an endearment.

'You will learn this about me: I am not a man who will be intimidated by any ghost from your past writing some sick letter.' His upper body rocked back and forth as he attempted to convince himself. 'This,' he held his ridiculous piece of paper in the air, 'this only makes me more determined to protect you.'

III

The arched window buckled the trees outside as I walked up the staircase and carefully shut the bedroom door behind me. From the white dressing table I took the matching white chair and wedged it under the doorknob. I sat on the edge of the bed. I sat completely still and closed my eyes.

I'd underestimated Alexander. What was worse, he knew it. I had made the oldest of mistakes: every real prostitute must know that the dullest clients have the deepest fantasies – the most wholesome are also the most dangerous.

Reading his letter, feeling startled, feeling sick, I had also been strangely unsurprised.

This one afternoon had changed everything between us: we were in a small inner-city terrace house built for Victorian labourers but now painted a colour titled *Thoroughbred,* with a landscaped, water-featured, metre-square porch – and a million-dollars-plus price tag. The lawyers who owned it were having a baby and needed to expand. One lawyer was evidently an amateur photographer – on each sleek wall was a just-in-focus picture of the couple, say, standing by an Asian temple at sunset, or a market cart of tropical vegetables. Alexander and I had just finished up on their organic cotton bedspread and were lying side by side.

'I suppose you're going out now?' Alexander asked.

'Possibly.' Although I had nowhere to go and most likely would return to the flat above my uncle's garage to watch too many episodes of some television series.

'I can imagine you at a gallery, at an art opening.' He was staring at the ceiling, convivial; broken open slightly by the sex. 'All of you standing around discussing the brushstrokes.' Alexander turned, damp curls flattened on his forehead. 'Or perhaps you have another appointment?'

Probably I looked surprised.

'I don't want you to meet him.'

I paused. 'But I have to.'

'No.'

Dusk was settling outside, a blackbird sang in a plane tree. We both waited, curious to see what the other would do next.

'I'll pay you more to stay here with me.'

'The client will be waiting, Alexander. I can't just cancel.'

'I need you to.'

Sighing, but with my heart beating faster, I took my phone into the bathroom and locked the door. The lawyers were on vacation until the auction, and I was not expected back at the office that afternoon. Standing there, flushed pink in the mirror, I made apologetic noises into the phone as the scent we'd made rose off my skin.

'I shouldn't have done that,' I announced, returning to the bedroom. 'It was very unprofessional.'

'Was he upset?'

'He certainly wasn't pleased.'

Alexander was sitting up on the bed, batik pillows crammed behind him. Leaning down to the floor, to his inside-out trousers, he untangled his wallet. 'You charge us both the same amount?'

'Yes, I do.'

He doubled this sum and, biting his lip, handed it to me, unable to meet my eye.

Above the bed there were framed photographs of the owners' trip to Morocco, close-ups of a tiled wall, a minaret, a fountain in a courtyard. It would be too much to claim the images were transporting, but as the sun went down we were on the towel I'd spread out, and suddenly it was like every other time we'd met had been a preamble for this meeting. Our skin, already sweat-lined, slightly bruised, wanted to press closer, as close as possible – and a question hung in the air. I can't remember now if he asked it aloud, or if I guessed that he wanted to: What do you do for him, this man you're no longer meeting, and what does he do to you?

I leaned against Alexander and into his ear started talking.

After this session, when we met I would tell him some story about an imaginary client, and soon he'd be acting as whoever I dreamt up, doing what these characters supposedly liked to do. The style of apartment we were in determined the scripts he heard; according to the layout or décor, vivid scenes came to me. I suppose we did things the people who lived in the houses might have done. A couch with floral upholstery inspired one set of manoeuvres, a bold stripe shifted the mood and tempo.

Even if my accompanying storylines were as generic as the bleached pine we were often surrounded by – for I don't pretend to be a brilliant or inventive pornographer – these episodes stayed with me, unlike other couplings I'd had. Small details about the wallpaper or furnishings that the owners had chosen imprinted, and so, therefore, did the encounter. This total recall had made what we did addictive. But each episode locked into my brain was now shot through with horror. And I *wanted* to forget them. For Alexander must have left me and at some point on his long drive home, feeling the drug of our liaison wearing off, started composing a letter.

Forcing myself to stand from the bed I walked to the window and stared out at the horizon – the beckoning horizon. My packed suitcase: I did not need it. I could replace the clothes. I doubted I would want to wear them again anyway. I did not need my handbag. I'd just take the cash and my credit card and leave the rest. The engagement ring could stay on the bedside table in its leather box.

In which direction should I run? I calculated the safest path, trying to retrace the route from the house to the road. There was a bank of European trees that stopped abruptly where the garden ended and fields began. If I left now he would come looking and, in such wide open spaces, have little trouble finding me. If I waited until nightfall, I could travel across the fields parallel to the driveway with the aim of making it to the public road. There would be fences, of course, and cattle, and dogs – and I had no idea how long it would take to walk to the nearest town. Was there a moon? I hadn't noticed any moon. A sick feeling of treading through blackness washed over me.

Lines from that letter now slithered back: *a nymphomaniac . . . controlling her own constant, sick desire . . . someone who is frozen inside and only her price tag stops her rutting. She wants it all the time . . .*

I caught sight of Alexander striding across the lawn, his jacket collar turned up, his long frame pitched forward as he scowled at the grass. He was holding a bucket in his hands – the yellow bucket from the kitchen – heading towards the kennels, where the dogs were already on their hind legs, stretched up against the mesh doors, barking. Alexander opened the doors one by one, and taking the bird's wet innards from the bucket threw them inside: his fiends whipped round, crazed for these lumps and scraps of meat.

I went to the door and took away the white chair.

The hallway was dark, all shadows and angles, and my eyes were slow to adjust. Each closed door seemed blank and knowing. A scream waited in my throat – I swallowed it down, and turned the nearest door handle.

In this pale-blue room waited the outline of a man.

I reeled back: on a coathanger hung Alexander's dark-grey, beautifully cut silhouette. The suit was suspended from the window frame. A pair of polished black shoes waited underneath. Otherwise it was fastidiously swept of personal detail. No paintings on the wall, no photographs; not a book by the single bed. It was horrible to know he'd been lying on the other side of the wall to me, thinking up his next move.

There was no telephone.

Back in the hallway, I opened the door opposite. Drawn curtains – dark and stuffy. Feeling for a switch, I knocked a frame sideways. The light came on, revealing two single beds in old chenille covers, surrounded by piles of colonial detritus: boxes overflowing with stacks of pictures, rolls of plans, legal documents – I caught the word 'Executor' – and balanced on top of them an old dinner gong, and a beaded ceremonial shield. In the corner was a collection of light wooden spears, as basic and functional as a weapon could be. Local Aborigines, I supposed. No telephone.

More rooms were virtually empty but for old beds, each one carefully made up with ageing linen: ready for Alexander's heirs . . . heirs I was meant to provide. Occasionally, against a bare white wall, stood an antique, a cabinet or washstand of some intricacy, objects of luxury in the midst of the spartan, which drew attention to what must have been missing. I guessed the rest had been taken away and sold.

Still no telephone.

In the hallway again, each door seemed identical. A few were open that I was sure I'd closed. Hesitating, I listened – the deep silence of this house. I waited for my breath to steady, and the house seemed to wait too.

At the end of the hall three steps led to a smaller door that appeared to have been added later. The door had a stained-glass panel showing a tree of life with perfect round fruit. Attached was a lock that had in part been painted over. I pushed hard at its little bolt and shoved the door open. The smell, then, of mould.

It was another wing: the house repeated in shadow, a warren with lower ceilings and walls scarred by water damage. Paint was peeling in great swathes, chunks of plasterwork had broken off. This was the part of the house I'd seen from the back, the ad-hoc extension like a series of strange growths. These rooms were connected to the downstairs kitchen area by a narrow staircase. The servants had worked there but lived up here. They'd been gone for thirty or forty years – leaving cheap, plain furniture stacked in corners, dust, dead insects, mouse dirt – but it felt as though they'd only just closed the door and fled, their departure somehow connected to Alexander's madness.

When I'd told him I was leaving the country, he seemed to take it as a personal affront. 'What aren't you happy with?' he'd asked accusingly, implying this set-up between us was without fault or complication. The next time he rang to make an appointment he kept me on the phone for longer, and there was more need in his goodbye. Then, at our subsequent meeting, he began asking questions, questions regarding my past. What school did I go to? Did I like it? Was I a good student? What is Norwich like? And the neighbourhood where I'd grown up? Could I see myself ever returning there? 'I hope not,' I'd answered.

I glanced in at the servants' bathroom; a piece of lace beige with dust was nailed over a small window. In the next room, a rusting bed frame and putrid mattress, biblical in age, were positioned beneath a plastic crucifix and a hand-stencilled sign: GOD IS LOVE.

In the kitchenette, hanging on the oven's handle, a tea towel was long shrivelled. I stopped, and for a second the towel seemed to sway. Here, in the middle of these endless fields, there had been people, meals cooked, children playing around the people cooking. The towel was stayed again.

Turning, I glimpsed a telephone, an old black Bakelite with finger dials, fixed to the wall. I swooped on it even though I knew it was surely long disconnected. I held the dusty receiver to my ear and listened to nothing. Only a sound like that in a shell which one might pretend was the sea, or the last murmurs of an extinct species. People who vanished when they were of no further use.

'Will you give me a photo of yourself?' Alexander had asked a few weeks earlier. 'For after you've gone?'

I presumed he wanted nudity. 'I don't think I have any.'

'Not even from when you were younger?'

'No.'

'A school photo?'

'They're all locked away back in England, thank God.'

'Well, it's not like I can't imagine what you were like.' He said this in a way that annoyed me. 'And I'm sure if I went looking I could find your picture *somewhere*.'

We were lying on the hardwood floor of a weatherboard bungalow with sea views. His hour was up but his arm was still stretched over me. Often he'd been slightly surly when our sessions ended, and now there was something else – resentment.

'Do you feel perhaps you had a duty of care to that guy?'

I was gently patting the floorboards, checking for a dropped earring. 'Which guy?'

'The one watching.'

'Watching who?'

'You – watching you with his girlfriend.'

I understood. Alexander had arrived at this address just as I finished showing the house to a young couple. Later, he asked what they'd wanted and I reworked a story involving a voyeur, a script we'd used before, when it was fun. 'Are you worried about him?'

'No, but I mean, I doubt seeing *you* do all those things made him feel good.'

'It was what he asked for. He'd requested it.'

'Still.'

We needed to get out of this house before the vendor's babysitter brought her twins back from kindergarten. 'I suppose at the time his self-esteem didn't seem like my problem, okay?'

'Do you ever wonder what happens later, when your clients leave?' He sounded genuinely angry.

As far as I was concerned the phantoms we discussed vanished the moment I took the towel out from beneath us and stuffed it in my bag. 'To be honest,' I answered, 'I don't give it a lot of thought.'

Nodding: 'So, it's just business to you?'

Amongst his new lines of enquiry would there now be the ethics, if you will, of prostitution? The responsibilities and obligations a sex worker might have to her clientele? He had never again asked me not to meet another man, or offered to pay extra for exclusivity. I'd assumed he knew there was no need.

In the kitchenette I shut my eyes, trying to keep the layout of his house in my head. I had been trained to draft floor plans, but these small rooms had no logic to them. They were designed to switch off a person's spatial sense, to completely disorientate.

Hearing something rattle, I glanced behind me. Nothing.

. . . You will be pulled down by her, pulled down all the way . . .
by someone who is frozen . . . sick . . .

I peered into the narrow rooms on either side. Each time I turned I felt something shift on the periphery. It was the fusing of dust and the very idea of being trapped in here, the house's dankest part. Unable to stand the thought, I moved like a bird banging into glass, trying to get out.

Now I couldn't even find the door, the tree-of-life door, and when finally I rounded a corner and saw it, no reflection came from the other side, the glass was so dull with grime. Again the door stuck, and again I had to push and pull it until I was back in the Colquhouns' forest-green hallway. Shaking, the adrenalin thudding through my body, I realised there was one last room I hadn't checked.

The crystal doorknob was faceted like the diamond I did not want.

Turning it, I walked into a large and bright and cold master bedroom. A row of tall sash windows gave a prime view of the dilapidated garden – the hedged rose garden at its centre – and the acres of encroaching farmland. It was a scene blasted back on itself by the mirrored doors of an elaborately carved wardrobe. These doors also repeated the thick, floor-to-ceiling chintz curtains and matching bedspread, patterned with bouquets, great fistfuls of bleached-out lilac, which seemed straight out of an interior-decorating magazine circa 1985. All of it – even the regret – was a scene trapped in amber. I stood there frozen too. The room was powerfully feminine and I began to shiver.

I walked over to the nearest bedside cabinet. I'm not sure why, but I reached out to touch the woman's silver hairbrush and matching hand mirror. Near them, a pair of fashionable reading glasses sat on a small tortoiseshell tray, and a book on Italian gardens was waiting to be read; resting upon it, a vase held a sprig with pale pink flowers.

I stepped back and noticed that just next to the cabinet, pushed against the wall, was a blue nylon-covered chair with thin plastic legs. The seat was very deep. The back was very high and straight, not unlike a chair they might have in a hospital. Then I saw the chamber pot beneath the seat.

The air became less breathable.

I glanced behind the first cabinet, trying not to disturb the little shrine, checking whether there were phone jacks in the wall, if there was any sign of a cord. Moving around the bed as though this place were wired, I went to the second, matching cabinet. Here, there was a glass.

It had water in it. Half crazed, I picked it up and drank.

This was where Alexander slept, I realised. The other bedroom down the hallway must have been his growing up, and perhaps he kept his best suit there, but he slept here. For now I noticed his money clip and cufflinks by the glass. As I scanned the room, I saw he'd moved the woman's things to the back on the dressing table and chest of drawers. His effects were neatly arranged at the front.

Unlike elsewhere in the house, there was no dust on any of these belongings. It wasn't like they'd been left untouched. The arrangement was *meant* to be this way.

I went to the wardrobe, towards my own reflection, and opened the doors. Why did I do this? Even glancing inside, inhaling camphor, I knew I wouldn't find a telephone, but I suppose I was now looking for something else. A clue to set me free. At one end of the wardrobe were Alexander's trousers and jackets – a careful palette of grey, navy – and at the other, a range of women's clothes.

They looked expensive but out of date (although from the style it was difficult to tell their age, or that of the petite woman to whom they belonged). Some of the clothes seemed to be decades old, but when I studied them more closely, lifting the drycleaner's plastic wrapping, it was hard to say if I was taking in a silk dress from the 1980s or a modern version of a vintage dress, whether they were from before or after his mother had passed away. Skirts, blouses, and even women's jeans were folded over wire hangers. A good deal of the clothes looked – what was the right word? My mother would call them *racy*: low cut, sequinned, sometimes slightly sheer. They were the clothes of someone very aware of her physical presence.

I had no blueprint of Alexander Colquhoun's past; no idea in which corners the ghosts were, or who they were. I did not know whether he had always lived in this house alone, or if another woman had shared it with him – even another fiancée. The one thing I could sense for sure was that no other woman was here now.

Off this bedroom was an ensuite bathroom.

It was straight out of the 1950s, tiled mint and mauve. A boom-time renovation, probably, in deco-revival style . . . I was on the edge of hysteria, but still scanning the décor for my clue: the toilet and basin and recessed bath were all in matching mauve enamel, the bath itself set into the wall like a stage with a proscenium arch, the taps in the shape of serpents ready to disgorge water. This eye of mine, I couldn't switch it off.

On the vanity were cut-crystal bottles and jars: a set a young bride might have received as a wedding present. They too were all pushed in careful rows to the back, replaced by a generic anti-dandruff shampoo, RapidShave, a Gillette razor.

A mirrored cabinet hung over the basin. I opened its doors.

On the top shelf were the usual unisex things: scissors, antiseptic cream, an uncoiled bandage. He'd need these if someone scratched or bit him.

The makeup on the bottom shelf was cheap. Covergirl foundation the sick orange colour of rotten fruit congealed in a plastic tube. A darker, mocha-hued face powder in a jar had been spilt and now covered everything else like ash: the boxes of eye shadow and little compacts of blush. I reached in and picked out a lipstick, an old bright scarlet, then I picked a recent brand, marked 'Island Dawn', a light pink, only used once or twice. And this is the thing that got to me: it was makeup from different times, for women with different skin-tones, and tastes and budgets.

In the basin below the cabinet, a tap dripped.

A rust stain ran from the tap to the plughole.

I doubled over, ready to retch.

Stumbling back to the bedroom, I saw in the wardrobe's mirrored doors the empty green garden behind my own pale face. Turning to the high windows I sensed Alexander was no longer outside. He was back in the house and I had to get out of this room.

In the hallway I put my hand to the steep railing and rushed down the stairs. Shafts of light played complex spools of grit on the landing. I turned and moved faster. When my feet hit the tiled floor of the entrance hall, I went straight to his office. That's where his phone had to be, I thought, although I hadn't noticed it the day before. He'd called me once a week to make an appointment, and I'd called him to accept his invitation here. I looked around at the filing cabinet, the bookcases, then back at the leather-lined desk. The computer screen was blank. No clouds now, the outside world had been switched off. Any telephone removed.

I stood fixed to the spot, and I remembered just yesterday finding his pile of letters.

Inside the desk drawer the envelopes were waiting, all with his name in the old-fashioned script. There were about eight of them – one for every week since Alexander's offer had arrived. They'd been postmarked in places I recognised from working at the estate agency – suburbs where I'd scheduled appointments with Alexander. Had he brought the letters to our meetings, then found the nearest mailbox?

The first few started out polite, with just a few disapproving lines about my being on the make, then they turned into longer rants. For the author, the writing of them seemed to have become recreational – and almost confessional. They were full of a strange kind of private bile, a toxic stream of consciousness.

Riffling through them, I read:

. . . the great slut up against fences on Saturday nights, all the kids practically cheering . . .

And then:

. . . she never charged me much and some guys just swapped some junky thing, a 50p trinket or a perfume sample . . .

I heard myself howling without even realising I'd opened my mouth.

. . . these freaks did weird sick things with her. They were her ideas, it excited her. Always a bit further, a bit further. Then it got dangerous . . .

I saw a reflection in the window and turned.

'Are you looking for something?' He was standing in the doorway.

'A telephone.'

'Why?'

'I want to call a car.'

He stared at me.

'I want to leave.' The voice that was mine now broke with fear. 'Please, just let me go.'

Nothing – Alexander seemed to not hear me. I kept pleading, and he kept staring back with infuriating blankness. The two of us were separated by something impenetrable. I flew at him, furious at every cent I had taken, at every sold and bought moment built up between us.

'It isn't true!' I screamed, throwing my whole body into hurting him. My hands. My nails. My teeth. But resistance only heightened his enjoyment, and wrestling the knot, I tightened it.

IV

'They've been coming for nearly two months. That first letter I found one evening, after returning from seeing you. I parked on the roadside by the mailbox and it was waiting there. I thought it was some prank.'

Alexander's speech had become slow and mechanical, each sentence cranked from deep within.

'I even looked around to see if the person who wrote it was watching me. I've never, ever felt anxious before on this land and now I was glancing over my shoulder. On my own land. I'd be out checking the stock, not a soul in sight, and my heart would start pounding. And I'd get back into the truck, get in and just drive, drive and try to breathe. When I left here to do shopping, I'd walk along the main street watching men I've known all my life, wondering whether one of them had written it.'

He paused, turning to me, his face now grey. 'But how could they have known? I had not told anyone I was seeing you.'

We were in the pink bedroom with the ring box still on the

side table. The air smelt of sweat: I wasn't sure if it was him or me – or the room itself. After our fight, after realising I wouldn't be permitted a phone call, I'd come back upstairs for the envelope of money, and within minutes he had followed me. He was sitting on the edge of the bed, his head in his hands.

'Liese, I'd speak to people about the weather, about grain prices – *Oh, yes, tough year, tough year* – and I'd be watching them for some sign they'd heard about us. Were they sneering? Were they trying to get away?

'I ran into a couple a few weeks ago who live forty kilometres from here – it's a good property, I went to school with him – and they seemed to look at me differently, as if they'd been told something. Usually they invite me for a meal, not that I want to go. The wife always tries to set me up with some large schoolfriend of hers – but this time they didn't mention dinner. She was curt. Without her knowing I intended to propose, I imagine she'd think I was taking advantage, treating you like you were just dispensable . . .'

He was shaking his head. 'Everyone – the station manager and his slag wife, the vet acting all matesy, even that bitch who runs what she calls "Providore", her grandmother was a maid here – I wondered if they knew.

'I mean, surely you get the picture? There are people in this district who'd get no greater pleasure than bringing down a Colquhoun . . . You think it's amusing, I know you do, but all my life they've been spreading rumours about my family. It's a favourite local pastime.' His mouth, set tight, was tasting an old, bitter ingredient. 'Basically my parents became "characters", their fights the stuff of gossip: once, she threw him out, and he returned with a locksmith and had the locks changed before throwing *her* out. She didn't even have a shopping bag of clothes, and this was a woman who was very proud of her appearance. Well, then he broadcast to the world all the details of her illness.'

'Was it the same illness?' I pictured the commode down the hallway.

'Yes, her head.' He tapped at his own.

'A second letter came about a week later, and this one's tone was different. I thought of mentioning it, but to be honest, when we met I was watching you.'

In the sunlit apartments he'd sometimes gaze at me with a kind of remorse, like a man coming to, wondering if he'd made a bad mistake. Now he brushed his hand over his face to wipe this expression off.

'It's terrible to admit, isn't it? I was watching to see if this was a scam of yours. I assumed whoever had been writing was working up to blackmail. Did all your clients receive something similar? It would be a nice sideline to the prostitution, clever . . .' He seemed to half test the theory. 'I wondered if you'd taken photographs of me, of us. This makes me sick to say aloud, but I'd started checking the rooms for hidden cameras. Once, when you were in the bathroom, I even looked through your phone.' He glanced up. 'Did you know that?'

Visualising it sent a pain behind my eyes. 'No.'

'I didn't find anything.'

'No,' I said again, fully realising now that he believed every mad word of his story. That was the most frightening thing, the way he was discussing this, his conviction. I no longer had a sense that he was augmenting some fantasy. I had no sense that this was even sexual for him – the letters seemed to be anything but a turn-on. He was scared by them.

'By the time I got the third one, well, I was angry. It was pornographic, vile, and yet, Liese – this is strange – it didn't put me off. Funny, isn't it? If anything, it heightened the attraction – and also, I suppose, my resolve to help you. It's hard to meet compatible people. I already felt strongly for you, very strongly, and the idea of taking things further then came to mind: why not marry her?'

Alexander shared his insight with a kind of proud wonderment, for a moment enjoying outwitting the letter's author. 'All I want, all I've ever really wanted is to live quietly, for no one to even notice me . . . to notice *us* now. I mean, I imagine that would suit you too? A life far from your past?'

He shifted his weight and the bed creaked. 'It will be a chance for both of us to start again. You –' his expression verged on desperation, but I could not tell if it was desperate love or a desperate desire to control me – 'you are the one. I've had my chances with *nice* girls,' he used the word sneeringly, 'and it always turns out they don't really understand me.'

The women's possessions in his bedroom flashed through my head, the clothes hanging behind thin plastic, the makeup stiffening on the cabinet shelf. And then I thought of the servants' quarters with its stained walls.

'I knew going into our engagement it wouldn't always be smooth sailing.' Alexander shrugged. 'I suspected you had something painful in your past you didn't want to face. One day you might trust me enough to tell me what it is.' Nodding, reassuring himself. 'What I'm getting at is, you don't have to keep doing this any more. I'm setting you free!'

My mouth was dry. There seemed nothing I could say.

Past him, out the window, I could see the cypress pine's branches moving, spirals of needles twisting in the wind. The idea of hiding the money on my body and walking away from this house now seemed naïve.

'When I was researching your line of work,' he reminded me, 'I found out some terrible things. I don't need to tell you there are a lot of bigots out in the world, real sickos who can't have normal relationships with women.' He shook his head. 'Whoever wrote these letters evidently needs to debase prostitutes any way he can.' Alexander frowned, thinking carefully. 'I suppose if she's just a piece of meat, this man feels all-powerful, or avenged, or whole – that's the two-dollar theory, anyway.

'Every time I see a newspaper story now about some girl's body found in bushland, I'm driven crazy imagining such a thing might happen to you. I've always hated men who hate women.' He looked my way, vehemence making his features sharper. 'Mum had depression, and sure, sometimes she behaved embarrassingly. Perhaps she drank too much but she was kind. All my father ever did was bully her.'

The tree slowly waved through the glass.

'Liese, earlier, in the kitchen, you told me that perhaps the letters' author was wounded, that he needed help.' Alexander's tone was full of mock sympathy. 'I've got no patience for that sort of horseshit. This business of "Oh, he had such a difficult childhood" excusing bad behaviour, it's ridiculous. And I should know. The man who wrote these letters is a pervert. Nothing else, okay? I want you to take this seriously because he may even be dangerous. Until we find him, I will come into the house and check on you on the hour if I need to. That's a vow. I will check on you by CB radio every half-hour and you will tell me you are safe. If *ever* he comes near you again,' his teeth were clenched, 'I don't care, I won't hesitate, I will kill him!'

'Did the first letter come after I told you I was leaving the country?'

Alexander regarded me blankly; my seeming calm was the wrong reaction.

'Or was it before?'

He thought about this. 'Before.'

'Really?'

'No, no, wait! You're right, it was after. Just a day or so after.'

The connection was so blatant I don't know how he managed to keep up the front. Panicked by the idea of my departure, he'd created this 'evidence' about my past, the past he wanted me to have, to justify making me his ridiculous wife-cum-whore-cum-slave. But the letters were also props to elevate the drama. And it followed that I was supposed to play along, to act frightened so he could storm around then offer me protection.

'I wondered, actually, if this was your pimp writing.'

'My pimp, is that so?'

'I thought you must have left him in the lurch, gone out on your own, and now he's sort of taking his revenge.'

Alexander leaned forward, the collar of his rugby top turned up almost jauntily, his fingers arranged in a thick-knuckled steeple. 'We need to look at this from every angle. If you have to tell me about all the clients – the abusers, really – that you've ever had, what each of them wanted in all its detail, that's okay.' His expression was one of bravery. 'I'm not saying it won't be painful, but I'm prepared to do it.'

'No. I don't think so.'

'Consider it a game. You like games.'

I shut my eyes. *Dear Nightmare, why?*

'Too many to recall?' He exhaled. 'Together we can work it out, who it will be.'

'*Will be?*'

'It will be someone you saw more than once.'

No one. There was no one but him.

'Perhaps it was that man who liked to . . .' He broke off. 'You remember . . . *that* thing.'

Who was he talking about? What had I told him?

As Alexander waited his face turned taunting. 'Liese, you *know*, don't you? You know who's been writing?'

It was exciting playing detective, and he would not back down. 'You suspect?'

I could barely look him in the eye. 'Yes, I do.'

'If I showed you these letters . . .' He reached inside his jacket pocket. He had brought the correspondence upstairs with him. And he'd obviously intended this to be as disturbing as possible. 'No.' Vigorous head-shaking. 'No, I can't do it to you.'

As he talked about why the letters shouldn't be read, I watched his mouth moving, those plump lips that were wet with satisfaction, and I asked myself, How do prostitutes get fired?

They don't give good service, presumably. They don't laugh or moan or not look bored at the right time. They grimace at the sight of the man's age, or his girth. They say his name as if it's a chastisement, a joke, like his wife does. They humiliate him. They don't humiliate him enough. They complain about the money: it's too little, or – and something now exploded behind my eyes – or, in very rare cases, it's too much.

Alexander was still talking, but I got up off the bed and started to unbutton my blouse. I felt the cool of the room on my skin, on the sides of my arms and chest. Around us hung a series of framed prints showing flowers with fairies hiding near the stamens, on the stems. Delicately I unzipped my jeans. I pulled them down and stepped out of them in a way that was meant to be balletic. On my body the bra and knickers became small strips of burgundy lace – a gesture, really, towards the concept of underwear, a homage. He stopped to look at me. To really look.

'Liese, have you been listening?' he said. 'You don't have to do this any more.'

Something in his voice, however, suggested I might actually need to do it just one last time. Reaching out, I took his hand. Such a thin man, the model ectomorph but with hands warped from farm work, covered in raised veins and now with red under his fingernails after gutting the bird. I no longer wanted to be touched by him, but I placed this hand on my skin.

I felt him tremble.

Before when he'd moved his fingers over my body, I wasn't

frightened of him. Now they crept lower slowly, very slowly, and I tried not to flinch. His rough fingers were beneath the fabric of my underwear. He closed his eyes.

A draught coming from a gap between the window's frame and its ledge made the curtains drift an inch, then back again.

I'd be doing a rental inspection, assessing the state of a tenant's curtains, of the carpets, walls, bathroom fittings; marking their state on a form from one to ten – ten being the least putrid – admonishing some rich girl whose parents paid her rent about the upkeep of the toilet, all the while recalling the time Alexander and I had spent in this very flat, contemplating what had happened, and what might happen in the next place. It was all I could think about.

We would be on the bed, or couch, or floor, and sometimes I wouldn't have any story prepared for him. I'd even wonder whether we should try silence, but then he'd start asking whether I had anything I ought to tell him – 'You don't want to hear.' 'I do.' 'Are you sure?' Often I would begin my confession still without an idea of what to confess. I knew the names of the people who owned the houses and so once or twice I even adopted the sexual personas I imagined they had. Someone with every inch of mattress covered in lace pillows would talk differently in the act of love, and want different things, to someone who, say, had a futon in a room painted deep turquoise.

Occasionally other people's belongings also became our props: once during sex I was arranged in such a way it was possible to reach out and open the drawer of a mirrored bedside table. It was as though I'd intuited the toys would be towards the back, but

I left the latex and baubles, instead pulling out a large feather, which I used in my story to some effect.

Steadily the things my imaginary clients liked to do became a wild half-guessing of Alexander's desires, and the fulfilment of my own. Certain characters with very specific requirements reappeared in my tales. Their needs were extensive, and Alexander liked to hear about them blow by blow, so to speak. One client might have a favourite body part, another turn out to be obsessed with a series of positions, and a third need some combination of angles, rhythm and textures that, I have to admit, touched on genius. Then, when every possibility seemed exhausted, there came a john who liked to use only his fingers, touching me in very much the way Alexander was doing now.

I took his hand off my skin and he opened his eyes.

He was gazing at me as if expecting I would start talking in our particular way, whispering in his ear a story of who he should be. Instead I went to my suitcase and unzipped the side pocket, taking out the envelope filled with cash. This was so obvious, why had I not realised earlier? The act of buying me, buying total control of me, was Alexander's real thrill. I pulled out half my weekend's fee. Clearly it wasn't the time to economise: I pulled out the other half.

'Here.' Turning, I presented him with every one of the hundred- and fifty-dollar notes.

He wouldn't touch it.

'I'm serious.'

He stared at the money, now splayed next to him on the bedside table, as though it were somehow disgusting. 'No.'

'Why not?'

'No.'

Forcing him wouldn't work. I'd learnt it was important to set up situations that made Alexander feel he had agency; made him feel that, despite my reporting on others' actions, it had still been his idea to take my underwear off with his teeth, and his idea, really, to then put his head between my legs. It was a fine balance, asking for things I wouldn't otherwise have known how to request, while never letting it appear I wanted this sex more than he did. In fact, it was better he thought I didn't want it at all, better to show only the mildest flicker of attraction, so that he felt like a man on the verge of primordial victory. Suddenly most of my clothes had disappeared and I seemed to be in a weaker position . . .

Anyway, this was what moved Alexander. Not my stripping to expensive but gaudy underwear, and kneeling in front of him – as I was now – wrestling him so as to undo his fly.

'Please!' I begged. It did not fit with the room we were in but I was no longer playing a character, this was *me*. 'Oh, please, let me, please . . .' For the strange thing was, suddenly I wanted him. I thought he was mad, and I no longer knew if I was doing this to attract or repel, but I wanted him; I was aching with some desperate mix of fear and confusion – and this desire.

The harder I pleaded, the more anguished he became. 'You don't have to do it any more.' He was holding his hands in the air. 'Liese, stop!'

Did Alexander require a piece of meat rather than a woman? Was he – as most men are – constitutionally threatened by too much female appetite? He liked hearing about what other men wanted, but preferred not knowing this was also what I craved.

For this craving, without the cash, seemed to cast me in a new light. It proved, I suppose, what he feared and revelled in most: the letter's claim that I prostituted myself for no other reason than pleasure.

And so he made a sound that was completely animal. A sound to empty his lungs of distress and fill them with rage.

I took my hands from his crotch, crawling fast away from him. Getting off my knees, I stood in the corner of the room, waiting. He was red-faced, breathing heavily, each long limb electrified and full of kick and hit. To reach my blouse and jeans I'd have to squeeze past him and I didn't want to be that close.

When his breathing slowed, Alexander stood and shook out his arms and legs, sloughing off my sleaziness. He picked up the suitcase, sighing. He pulled out my clothes and carefully refolded each garment, placing it in the white chest of drawers. Had he done this previously? When other women tried to leave? The routine seemed to calm him: his every gesture stayed measured, controlled. None of what I'd done had aroused him. Without the cash it couldn't.

'You know how I feel about you,' he said quietly. He leaned across to the bedside table and took the leather box, snapping it open. Inside was the diamond, bending light. It was my enemy. My beautiful enemy. I watched him slowly slide the ring over my finger.

'We will have to break this habit, Liese.' From his back pocket, Alexander was taking out his wallet. 'Now you are my fiancée, I can't allow you to see anyone else.'

I did not answer.

He removed five new hundred-dollar notes and laid them on top of the rest.

'The others will have to give you up.'

His extra money seemed to glow.

'And what might be more difficult,' he smiled ruefully, 'you will also have to give *them* up.'

I closed my eyes. The air in the room was richer, but I felt washed in hot shame. The horror was he knew how to activate something in me, drawing me further into his trap – a trap I couldn't help feeling I had laid for myself. This routine between us was my creation. I had sketched out its shape, and for months had lived under its shelter. But desires bend and stretch, and in the web of his mind, my imaginings had gone bad. *How can you leave?* my fiancé's eyes mocked. *How can you possibly escape your own fantasy?*

'Now,' Alexander ordered, 'read this.'

V

Dear Mr Colquhoun,

It comes to my attention you have not heeded my warning and ceased communication with Ms Campbell. I therefore feel obliged to bring certain aspects of her character to your attention. I have attached testimonials (a sample of dozens I've now collected) from her former acquaintances. Please see overleaf:

I turned the page. The first 'testimonial' was typed on cheap paper that had been handled a lot.

Some lads said she was up herself, acting posh, bragging about moving away. If they took too long she'd start making snoring noises and they'd get crapped off. Not me. I saw stars. Big girl with blonde hair, alright face, good body, charging £10 for a bareback

blowjob or £15 for a full service. She would do all
of it for a bargain £20. And once I heard in the upstairs room of the video store on Sander St she spent
three hours standing, sitting, squatting for like a
party of five or six, and she hardly charged extra . . .

The note continued in this vein and was signed with a fake
name and address that I assumed Alexander had chosen for effect:
Greg Blackwood, 44, Unthank Road, Norwich.

I turned another page:

We'd meet on the edge of the golf course. It was
dark but she had a torch which she flashed three
times, and I'd find her lying on the moist grass with
her burgundy school dress pulled up, her skin all
salt and sour, begging me to . . .

Several paragraphs detailed my 'hot wet slit' and its encounter
with a 'throbbing cum-rod'. Were these the things that turned
Alexander on? The stories I'd told him were far more subtle, far
classier. I needn't have bothered if this was what he preferred.
Pathetic little dirty stories which were almost comic – not that I
could now find a way to laugh.

. . . for a fiver there was a map you could buy from
the neighbourhood lads with a key to places around
the estate where she'd happily liaise.

Anonymous, Westlinks Rd

On the next page I saw a photocopy of a hand-drawn map showing twisting half-circle streets, marked with the following index:

1: golf course (at night.)
2: the lane running behind the houses backing onto Eaton Primary.
3: the school playground on the half tyres that make up the shite equipment.
4: the path parallel to Wentworth Green and adjoining oval. Go to gate with wire cut away.
5. her house, obviously.

My family's house was depicted in crude style, although the details were right. This meant Alexander knew where my parents lived.

How?

He had found the address. But how?

He had typed their street into the internet and up must have come the asphalt's potholes, a tree's shadow over those holes, every leaf on the tree. And past that, a little fence of rope strung between low posts, and the patches of front lawn that needed watering, my father's pink and white impatiens reflecting in the front windows of a red-brick, gable-roofed, two-storey house.

I felt a jolt like one I'd had at eighteen: I was sitting in the dark lecture hall, newly arrived at college, a projector on, the lecturer showing a slide of a house that he said epitomised bad, lazy, cynical design. And it was basically our family home on the screen. The house I'd grown up in on Wentworth Court. The other students were all laughing, although once my embarrassment faded I became sure they lived in similar places. It was the early 1990s, the ascendancy of Hadid, Gehry, Koolhaas and computer-aided design packages. In class everyone was morphing a 3D blob, stretching it one way, pulling it the other, then 'post-rationalising' the blob as a comment on fractal geometry or game theory. Anyone with style was supposed to reside in a comet tail, not dwellings like the one projected on the wall.

Pressing his little hand-held button, the lecturer had continued his slide show of lower-middle-class English kitsch: row after row of postwar, two-storey, single-garage houses, all basically the same but for a Tudor element here, a Georgian or Victorian touch there. He'd created a series of still lives out of the ghostly objects veiled by these houses' net curtains: studio portraits of long-grown children; a solitary armchair and reading lamp, the shade askew; maidenhair ferns; plastic daisies in a vase; figurines of angels, or swooning shipwrecked couples, or wigged aristocrats alighting carriages to masked balls. These places, with their *faux* period details and statuettes, were temples of Thatcherism. Tory-voting aspirants lived within. 'For a start all this should be bombed,' the lecturer pronounced, his scorn wedging inside me.

Alexander had seen exactly where I'd come from. On the computer, he must have spied through the windows at my family's belongings, into the living room where the impressionist posters hung next to photographs of my sister in her wedding dress, and now holding her baby. Nothing of provenance, nothing of permanence, but everything spotless. After thirty years, nearly all the houses in the neighbourhood looked as if the residents had only just moved in.

He had then clicked some arrow and zoomed out over the low fence, past the storybook trees and topiary hedges to the rest of Sunningdale Estate, a maze of cul-de-sacs named after the great golf courses of the world. Here people walked their dogs at three-quarter speed, cyclists pedalled in slow motion, and even the birds flew overhead as through some confection thicker than air: all of it seemed a kind of suburban asylum where everything was drugged . . . Alexander would have taken in the local golf course where my parents had memberships – hiding the clubs if their family, scornful of perceived climbing, visited – and a little further on a sports field with a path parallel to it. This path, which he'd referred to on his map, was the one I'd taken every day after school. Kids used it as a shortcut, the older ones smoking, or snogging, or doing lame graffiti on back fences. For a split second I felt something in my brain turn slightly.

Blackwood, that was a name on one of the testimonials – there were Blackwoods who lived around the corner from our house. They owned a copying business. All the family were heavy-set, a low centre of gravity . . . No. I shook my head to stir the image out.

'This is ridiculous!'

'Why?'

'Because,' I waved the letter in front of him, 'none of it ever happened.'

Alexander nodded slowly. 'Are you sure?'

He was still sitting on the single bed, hands knotted, shoulders slumped, trying to gauge the severity of my problems. 'I want you to think back and really concentrate, Liese.'

'Oh, come on,' I started, and then couldn't find words for the scale of this farce.

In the late eighties the trees on our estate were still saplings, and ornamentals anyway – if they grew too tall it would have been antisocial. I was visible everywhere I walked, everywhere I thought of walking. It was like God's own eyes were upon me. Each garden was just a little patch of open lawn, each neighbour's flowerbeds more perfect than the one before. Everyone was on view. There was nowhere to go and not be seen. And the safest place, the only place, to have sex was in your head.

> She told me that one day after school she was window-shopping on St Stephens Street when a woman approached her and asked if she wanted to make money. The woman, a madam, must have recognised her for the type who'd turn tricks in her spare time. Not just from her tarty clothes and makeup, but from her eyes because she looked like she wanted it all the time, and it was all she was good for. The madam had a brothel near Sweet Briar Road . . .

I spluttered.
'What's the matter?'
'A brothel! I didn't know there *was* a brothel in Norwich.'

. . . and it catered to people with obscure tastes –
it was a place for the real weird types. Sometimes
she'd tell me the things these freaks made her do,
she whispered them when we were together. Her
head had been reset, she liked now to be frightened.
Truly, it excited her, the edge of fear seemed to get
her going, made her feel something . . .

I knew Alexander was watching me. But I could not look up
from the page. I felt hot and cold. There followed a list of acts I'd
truly never thought of. The strange thing was that all this vapid
pornography, all the claims that I wanted to be hurt in these various
ways, affected me far less than his knowing real details about me:
the colour of my school uniform – what kind of creep would find
that out? – the street where I'd gone shopping as a teenager, the
half-tyres around the grounds of my old primary school.

'Was there play equipment in the area you grew up?' As our
weekend together approached, Alexander's questioning had
become increasingly off-kilter. He seemed to imagine I was from
some urban slum. 'Were there any sporting facilities? Any fields or
ovals that the local lads could use?'

He'd asked what I thought were trivial, if odd, questions about
my background, and he'd obviously used the answers as an aid to
further research.

I shook my head. It was as though he were trying to put me in
my place. As he drove me mad, he wanted me to remember where
I'd come from.

'How have you done this?' I now asked. He had not seemed

a particularly creative man.

'Done what?'

'Found this out, made up such filth.'

'Liese, try to calm down. You're not thinking clearly.'

I was still only half dressed – had he purposely waited until I was nearly naked to have me read his letters? I slapped the pages down next to him and covered myself with a blouse that I now buttoned haphazardly. I grabbed my jeans off the floor, stepping into them. My socks were caught in the jeans' legs. I leaned against the white bed end, putting them back on my feet as quickly as I could. This bastard wanted a bona fide whore with an anthology of sluttish vignettes for use at night, and enough shame to keep her servile throughout the day.

Alexander was watching me open a drawer he had just refilled, his expression close to pity. Sighing, he said, 'I think you're trying to avoid something.'

'And what would that be?'

'I think you act while in a kind of trance. That you, I don't know,' he rubbed at his forehead, 'that you're attempting to escape something painful.'

Was he actually going to head-shrink me, psychoanalyse my false identity? He hadn't come across his theories riding in his dung-splattered truck, talking to his cows. Were they remnants of his own failed treatment?

'It draws you in and you have to have sex. But you don't feel it. You don't feel anything.'

I chose a thick woollen top – if I found a way to get out of this house and walk towards safety, I didn't want to freeze. I lifted it over my head, and the engagement ring's platinum claw, the claw holding the diamond, got hooked and pulled at the wool. My head covered, I struggled to unsnag it. Finally I got the top down and slammed shut the drawer. The prissy white chest and its ornaments shuddered. Had he put me in this pink room as a rehabilitative measure? To 'give me back' my childhood?

'Sometimes, as a side effect of trauma, people have addictions, sexual ones.'

'That's very unfortunate for them.'

'It's treatable.'

I was sitting on the floor, pulling on my running shoes, lacing them. 'You shouldn't believe everything you read on the internet, Alexander.'

'Liese, we can face this. The doubts you have, the insecurities, there's no need. I love you . . .' He leaned forward, his blue eyes now awash with tenderness. And soon he was next to me on all fours, reaching out as though to a scared animal. His not shaving had begun to make him look older. 'I want you to feel you can talk about this with me.'

'Wow, thanks.'

'From now on, if you have a problem, it's a problem for both of us, darling.'

'Why does that sound like a threat?' As I stood I realised I wasn't only frightened, now I also hated this man, hated his oppressive sincerity, and retrieving the pile of letters I threw them in his face.

'Okay . . .' Alexander kneeled to bundle the papers. He was strenuously maintaining his calm, even as he gathered up the last page. Straightening, he stared at it and asked casually, 'Were you close to any teachers at school?'

'What's that supposed to mean?'

'Oh,' a small shrug of defeat, 'nothing.'

I grabbed the page out of his hands, knowing that I should not keep reading; it encouraged him and fed my own warped fascination, growing now exponentially like some cursed seed.

> . . . perhaps it was wrong to do it, but she was no longer my student. And if it wasn't me it would have been someone else who might not have been so caring . . .

My mistake was to not regard this as pure fiction: instead I started running through the teachers at school, wondering who he meant me to imagine this was – and each candidate was nauseating.

> . . . I answered an advert and I met her in the Holiday Inn on Ipswich Road just off the A47. She liked it because there was a glass door at the side facing onto the car park and you didn't have to walk through a foyer or security to get to the rooms. So I knock on her door and of course, I presume she recognises me, but she doesn't acknowledge it. For six years I've seen her across the classroom and not once does she say anything.
>
> This girl had every chance – I know because the parents turned up each time she or her sister ran a race or sang a song. She'd been quiet and studious,

until, I don't know, one weekend she must have watched *Pretty Woman* on video and next thing you know she's apparently the school's great slut – up against fences on Saturday nights, all the kids practically cheering. She was the toast of the staffroom each Monday morning.

One day she turns and asks me to do a certain thing that would hurt her and I didn't want to do it, not at all, but she'd asked for it and I'd have done anything for her. Well one thing led to another in that regard. It led to a lot of things, which most people would find too extreme.

I suppose I had the usual notions of how I'd leave my wife and she and I could move away somewhere warm and she would stop doing this. I was spending so much money. I was spending and spending. To see her I would go without eating or drinking out with friends.

But finally I realised she didn't want anything a normal girl would, only sex and cash. Each one got her as hot as the other.

This is very strange: I'd swear for her it was always the first time we'd met and I was always a stranger. I would dial her number and she would not remember me. Sometimes she'd pretend she did, but I knew it was an act. If I saw her in the morning I doubt she'd recognise me that afternoon. Did she see so many people she couldn't keep track?

I'd bring her gifts, expensive things that women like, and next time I would ask her about them and she'd look blank, or say something polite, humouring me, as if I was the one with a poor memory – and it made me wild, just really angry, and I tell you, I could understand then why men want to hurt whores and I didn't half wonder if in some cases they deserve it.

There was more, but I could not bear to keep reading.

I looked up at him, my fiancé. My eyes burned; everything around us seemed to be in extreme focus and I began to laugh. The room was giving way, the grain of the world turning coarse, and as I laughed I could feel myself falling. I had found the very edge of my life and now, too fast, I was descending.

VI

We were in his truck driving across the paddocks. How much later it was I did not know, but the day's colour was leaching from the horizon, making this place colder and greyer and more limitless. Alexander stopped by various gates and I climbed out. I tried to open their bolts efficiently, to not show that terror made my fingers slip on the cold metal, each lock a new test. No longer did I know what to believe. I did not trust the sky. Or the trees. Or the birds, invisible in the trees' darkening branches, their volume intense. I did not trust my own body, that my hands would do as I ordered. Wrestling with each gate, every field beyond looked just like the last, but with the slightest reconfiguration of trees and animals – two birds on a branch, then three – a kind of memory game.

Imagine someone coming to you and handing over a history of your life threaded with enough truth to make you wonder about the lies. *What have I done?* the letters were gnawing, *I don't understand what I have done.* They were fabrications, but whoever had written them seemed to know too much, to have access to information I could barely even recall.

Another gate, another bolt and latch connected to a thick steel chain: this one older and held together with pieces of rusting wire. The latch had a hole cut through it, and as I attempted to slide the hole at an angle over the head of the bolt, I could feel Alexander's eyes upon me. He watched from the driver's seat, in case I took flight across his fields. I tried to raise the whole gate and then unhook the latch. It would not give but my fingers kept trying, growing more clumsy, the engagement ring knocking against the steel.

Finally the gate came undone; I swung it wide and watched him drive through.

Shivering, I hesitated: I did not know where we were going, or why. What if I now ran and made it to the national park? Maybe he wouldn't find me. Maybe no one would. I had heard tales of children and foreigners getting lost in the bush. All around them the landscape must have looked the same, with no markers to distinguish where they'd just been — lost amongst all those trees that wanted to burn. A school-learned line from Emily Dickinson came back to me: *Dare you see a soul at the white heat?* No, I thought, I don't think I do. Those people never had enough water, and walked around and around in parched circles, slowly perishing.

I heaved the creaking gate closed, and again my fingers wrestled with the cold latch.

Back in the truck, Alexander said nothing. We'd barely spoken since he showed me the letters. I'd sat in my room feeling concussed while he stayed downstairs in the kitchen. But he had not been prepared to leave me in the house alone, and now he was giving off patience – stoic, aggressive, phoney patience – as he waited for me to admit my past.

I closed my eyes.

What if I had in fact stood against a back fence in a narrow lane, branches splayed above, and at my feet the build-up of leaves, while in the distance traffic sounded, then lights flicked on around the estate – a stranger's hands on the flesh of my hips?

What if I had been on the golf course at night, kneeling on the beautifully tended grass, unable to see the stars, to see anything with a belly in my face, fingers pulling at my hair?

What if I'd enjoyed it?

As we drove on, the trees moved back and forth, advancing, retreating, their outlines scrambled by mist.

'Wait a minute,' Alexander said to himself. 'Do not tell me.'

This paddock had an aluminium enclosure in one corner. The cow was lying here alone; in the distance other black calves and cows were stolid shadows.

Alexander muttered something under his breath. Parking the truck, he got out quickly, swearing. 'Do I have to check every tiny detail around here?'

I got out too.

'He should have told me she was ready. Useless fucking manager.'

Through the clumpy shitty ground, sinking further with each step, I followed as he approached the cow. Up close, the animal was shockingly big, bigger than anything I'd seen outside a zoo. From its vagina jutted two hoofs: two round segments of hard, striated bone, then thin ankles strung together, as if the creature were cross-legged inside the womb.

'It's all right, girl. It's all right.' Alexander's voice had changed slightly. He was stroking the animal's flank. 'It hurts, but you'll be all right.'

Coaxing the cow to its feet, he prodded it towards two vertical bars in the enclosure. 'Into the crush, come on, in you go.' He got his shoulder up under the cow, up under the protruding hoofs, and half heaved, half cajoled the cow into what he called the crush. There was an echoing clang as he slammed closed a hollow steel bar fixing in place the animal's neck. The cow blinked a huge sad eye.

'I'm going to have to pull it out,' Alexander announced, marching to the truck, taking a length of rope from the tray. Returning, he looped the rope around the calf's ankles then his own body, like he was lassoing himself. He drew it tight, leaning back so the rope took his weight.

'If you want to make yourself useful —' he started, irritated.

'Just tell me,' I snapped.

'Hold the tail out of the way.'

With fingers numb from the bolts and latches, I took the cow's tail, a sort of coarse tassel, and tried to look elsewhere. As Alexander began winching one creature from the other, I weighed up whether to make a run for it through his paddocks full of prize minotaurs, whether I'd be running from danger or towards it. While the letters scared me, what gave this fear an extra kick was the ungrounded guilt they aroused. It seemed clear who had written them, and yet I still kept thinking, Someone's found out about me, but he or she has found out things even I didn't know I'd done.

Into the silence a magpie made a warbling, talking call.

'Push!' Alexander urged tenderly. 'Push!' he pleaded, as gently he strained at the rope and the calf moved under the mother's hide and bone and muscle and meat. The cow bellowed and its legs gave way, the steel crush ringing as its head dropped down. Lying there, exhausted, the animal seemed to call out to the trees and the wind and the dusk, a deep guttural groan of oldest pain.

How could I have run?

With the cow collapsed, it was harder to pull the calf out. Alexander sank into soft wet ground. And soon he was actually sitting down in the mud, his knees bent in front of him, his torso forward, gripping the rope and pulling. He was strong, very strong, and slowly the calf emerged, its lower legs covered in oozing opalescent membrane.

The mother's vagina was stretched taut in all its raw elastic complexity, the pink of it unfolding before us. Again the cow bellowed, too alive now, and then the calf's haunches appeared.

'Push, push, girl!' Alexander now stood. 'Get up and push!'

I stared at him, and for the first time I thought I saw clearly who he was – the man I might have known if our first meeting had gone differently, if I had come to this place without charging a fee.

'It's alive!' Alexander called out, astonished. The cow seemed to be shuddering but it was the calf's lithe body moving from inside. 'The little bastard's alive!'

Alexander pulled harder, his whole face alight, and in one final wet heave, the calf came spilling out.

It lay on the ground, a black spineless thing with arms and legs outstretched. It seemed to have no eyes. It seemed to have no mouth. It swam in shiny black oil, twitching and wriggling inside a translucent sheath.

Alexander grabbed me in an awkward, almost teenage bear-hug. He clutched my shoulder, squeezing it, before breaking into an odd little two-step of joy. He was transported. And so was I. *Alive!* We too were alive! I had also been witness to the magic act, and a little voice asked me, Wait, what if this man's been telling you the truth? And then I thought, But if it's not him writing, who is it?

His arm was still over my shoulder. 'Why are you surprised it survived?' I asked.

'I've never seen a breech birth that's left waiting actually make it. They choke usually, choke on amniotic fluid.' Alexander bent down, gently unfolding the calf from the membrane as one might unwrap a parcel. Picking up the thin hind legs, he dragged the newborn beside the mother. He removed the restraints from the cow's head and prodded its flank with his boot, forcing the animal to stand. 'Time for work, girl.'

Heaving itself up, the cow gave a low, deep murmur, and sniffed at the calf, licked at it. Under the mother's great tongue, the calf's head moved. It flicked its new ears.

I found I was wiping my eyes.

Alexander checked that the cow had expelled the placenta, then, bending down, wiped the blood off his hands and wrists on a patch of grass. I stood watching the calf, stunned. The shining black newborn flung out its legs, learning how they worked.

When Alexander was done, he touched me gently on the arm and we walked to the truck. Dusk was swallowing the horizon, fixing my new need to keep glancing over my shoulder. It was just us, him and me and the animals. I felt a surge of tenderness towards him. I wanted to lay my head on his shoulder, to touch his hand. Watching this had broken me in some way, had broken through to something I hadn't known was closed over.

We both opened the truck doors and shut them at the same time; looking at each other, we shyly grinned. For a moment, just for the slightest moment, it was as though nothing bad had ever happened. And we were sitting in the near dark, watching as the gleaming calf knelt beside its mother, found a teat and drank.

The house smelled of Alexander's cooking: I followed him through the back door and into the kitchen, where he turned on the light to check the oven. The sink was laden with crockery, as if he'd used every utensil he could find. He cooked without bothering to tidy up, and on the work bench was a bowl of peeled and cored apples – he'd started filling the apples' centres with a red jelly from the food processor – alongside a pile of onion skins, a container of left-over stuffing, and the needle and thread with which he'd sewn the bird's vent after filling it. Nearby, *Larousse Gastronomique* was opened to 'Roast Goose with Fruit'. I was starving, but the odour of the roasting bird was intense, almost acrid.

Satisfied with the temperature, he strode out of the kitchen to another of the poky rooms off the servants' corridor. He pulled a cord and on flared a bare globe. This was the laundry.

I stood at the door averting my eye as he stripped off his birth-stained clothes. When he was just in a white singlet and a pair of boxer shorts, he turned on the groaning tap, and began brushing around his nails in the trough.

'Do you need help with dinner?' I asked.

'Oh no.' He glanced over at me. 'It's under control. Thank you.'

'I could do the dishes?'

'They won't take long. I'll do them later.'

I nodded, not wanting to push him. 'Well, I might go and freshen up. Unless you'd prefer to shower first?'

'No, after you.'

The shirt and jacket he'd lent me as well as my own jeans were covered in a less dramatic mix of mud and blood, but I didn't care. I felt light. Somehow I was managing to hold at a distance the unreality of the letters. And in doing so Alexander became almost an ally. It was easier to cope with being here if I believed there was someone out in the world, out in the darkness beyond this house, who wished us both ill – making him and me sudden innocents. Whoever had been writing was evil, but we were good people who worked on a farm. We helped animals, helped them and their babies. Perhaps it sounds mad, but I felt the flicker of a hope-filled truce open up between us.

'Liese.' Turning off the tap, Alexander put down his nailbrush. 'I have a surprise for you.'

Half laughing: 'Another?'

'Yes.'

'Well, I give in.' I smiled, waiting. 'Will you tell me what it is?'

'I'll show you.'

In his underwear, he led me through the corridor back to the entrance hall; his sinewy shoulders were tense, a stiff control had returned to his limbs. Pushing open the dining-room door, he revealed the long polished table to be decorated in lavish style, set with crystal wine and water glasses, monogrammed plates – cream with a cobalt trim and cursive *C* – and heavy silver cutlery, knives and forks of different sizes upon embroidered lace napkins. There must have been thousands, tens of thousands, of dollars' worth of family treasure laid out. It gave the table undeniable power. And posed a kind of dare: there were settings for six people.

He held himself very straight. 'I've invited a few friends to dinner.'

'Oh.'

'I wanted us to celebrate.'

Whereas an hour ago I would have instantly wondered which of the guests might rescue me, now I was also touched by the effort he had gone to. 'It looks beautiful.'

Alexander allowed himself a small grin. 'There should be flowers. Wait a minute.' He left the room and returned moments later with a pair of secateurs. 'Will you organise an arrangement?'

'Where from?'

'The garden, Liese.' He reached out, brushing my face. 'That's where flowers are made.'

Taking the key from the little hook behind the curtains, Alexander opened one of the room's French doors and stood back, evidently satisfied I would not start running.

On the veranda, inhaling the cool night air, I felt, for the first time in days, that I could actually breathe. The planting beds framing the lawn were lit by the dining room's windows and I cut a flower, a white camellia, the chill moving in and out of my lungs.

I cut another stem and stretched my neck, just slightly.

Soon this could be over. I had the option of asking one of the guests for a lift to the nearest town. There I could hire a car with the cash, and drive through the night to my old life – the idea was wonderful . . . And also not wonderful. My old life seemed increasingly frivolous.

I had lived too close to the surface – that was my job, making spaces easy on the eye. I had worked in artifice and illusion, convincing myself that finding the right stone, or marble, or colour of render to conceal some building's blemishes, was a useful way to spend one's days. Here I was connected to the things humans were meant to be connected to: cows and magpies and mud and dogs. I looked at the camellia bush, the buds set to open like perfectly wrapped gifts, each giving off the subtlest fragrance.

Probably I was just giddy, so close now to freedom, but I had to ask, What am I returning to? The flat above my uncle's garage? The daydream about China, where, in reality, I'd have to keep designing shiny boxes? Or, most likely – if I went home and tried to regroup – my old bedroom in Norwich, where every morning through the wall I'd hear the nozzle of the vacuum cleaner hit the doorframe, my mother's way of saying, Get out of bed! Start sending round your CV! I'd have to walk along our cul-de-sac to the post office, dodging the neighbours telling me how their sons-in-law had also been retrenched, knowing they still saw me as a big, plain lummox of a girl, not very popular and a bit standoffish. That was the irony of the letters: growing up, I had been the opposite of the neighbourhood slut. I'd been barely visible.

Those letters . . . They worked like a riddle at the edge of my brain.

I had not told anyone I was seeing Alexander.

He claimed he had not told anyone either.

If he had not written them, a third person was trying to drive one of us mad.

Was there anyone who could hate me that much?

Quite possibly. I'd left home at eighteen, and with a late bloomer's sheer will cured my accent, the slow-talking upswing, the provincial manners; I'd lost weight and learnt to walk and dress and even smile differently. The experiment had worked: I was desirable. And it was intoxicating to have this sudden power after the years with none. How ought I use it? One standard of feminine success came down to me from 1950s cinema, the heroines of those films sloughing off suitors as though it were a sport.

So yes, I could think of a number of men who at one stage or other would have liked to write me abusive letters, although most of them were now married with small children – they'd no longer have the time.

In Australia I'd effectively put myself in quarantine. Making Alexander pay for sex was meant to set up a firewall. The terms being clear, theoretically we could both gain considerable pleasure, without either of us getting hurt. However, I *had* come here to start a new life, and perhaps, despite our struggles, I was about to do it; to become a person who could commit to another. This new me would surrender. All these years, I'd believed that marriage extinguished identity. That it was a tether to the worst parts of someone else: their insecurities and vanities and futile emotional weather. But one can't avoid the horror of another person. A real person is horrifyingly, excruciatingly real! And yet – what real person does not want to fall to her knees with another in a great, ecstatic, transcendental show of giving up the self?

I looked around, making out, just, the edges of the hedged garden where Alexander had proposed. So, was I trapped? Who *isn't* trapped? If marriage was a trap, I had felt trapped outside the trap. Being forced into matrimony, being given this sort of nudge, was probably the only way I was actually going to do it.

I reached out to cut another camellia and focused on the sleeve of my jacket, my borrowed jacket. Alexander had left muck stains when, after the birth, he'd held me close. The sleeve's outer fabric was stiff oilskin, but it had a soft padded lining – and all at once this material felt different against my body.

Had he truly never solicited prostitutes prior to our meeting? His sexuality now seemed too complicated for a non-professional to have to deal with. Who had owned the assorted clothes I'd found upstairs if not other women? Well, my rational self explained, he is pragmatic: no point disposing of garments like this jacket that are perfectly useful. The day before, Alexander had also made me put on old clothes. He had watched me dress in another woman's shirt and trousers before we left the house to tour the farm. He had proposed to me, staring into my eyes with great longing, while I wore this outfit, and so, taking me in his arms, dancing, he'd inhaled someone else's perfume . . .

I cut another flower. These anonymous letters weren't a deflection from his own past, were they? There had been others here before me. Maybe he'd paid them, maybe he hadn't, but they had been kept in this house with him. And they'd left possessions behind, clothes and makeup, which he'd hung onto as mementoes. My chest was tightening: what if the letters regarding my ghosts blinded me to what was in plain view?

I stood, both hands holding a random bouquet.

'You are taking a long time.'

Alexander was standing on the veranda, observing me. Behind him the dining room's chandelier was ablaze, and through the French doors I could see the long table lined with plunder.

Freshly showered and dressed in clean clothes, Alexander came down into the garden. He firmly took the secateurs, then the pile of flowers out of my hands. His features were grey and shadowy. 'You've trimmed half the garden.'

I looked down at the stems I'd been holding – some were almost branches – and heard myself ask, 'Have you really never been married before?'

He began trimming leaves off the stems. 'No, I haven't.'

'Engaged before?'

There was a long pause.

'I thought our pasts weren't relevant, Liese?'

'But you've decided you know mine. So have you?'

He shook his head. 'Frankly, *you've* not really got any right to be jealous. None at all.' More quick, efficient cutting, then with his boot he swept the debris into a plant bed. 'You're trembling. Come back indoors.'

On the mahogany dining table there was now an elaborate tiered vase of silver and cut glass. He had chosen it to complement the rest of the table's spoils, but together these things looked awkward, as if in trying to recreate a memory from childhood, he'd tried too hard. Alexander transferred the camellias to the vase.

In the light, I noticed he had shaved. His skin was smooth again, except for a tiny nick to his cheek. I was standing next to him in another woman's clothes, and despite myself, despite every reservation, something in me caught. I was moved to kiss his wound, to show him real affection.

He blocked me, suspicious. 'What is it now?'

'Nothing!' I smiled, but felt foolish.

'The birth made you clucky. Is that it?'

'No!' I exclaimed. But *was* that it? That regardless of everything, I wanted life inside me?

'Arrange the flowers, please.'

The camellias were in the vase and there didn't seem much else I could do; I shifted around the stems.

Alexander crossed his arms. He seemed dismayed that the birth had brought out something base in me. 'A normal woman would see that and sex would be the last thing on her mind. Just about anything seems to get you started, though. It's lucky you *do* make me pay, Liese.'

I left the camellias as they were.

'No, no. It looks like you've found an old jam jar and stuffed them in. How hard can it be?' he asked, glaring at the arrangement. 'Isn't it a basic feminine art?'

'If you're displeased you can always fire me.'

He seemed genuinely surprised. 'What are you talking about?'
'Just fire me.'

Straightening, he stared at me with something close to loathing.
'No, I don't think it works like that. Til death do us part, et cetera.'

Why Alexander had suddenly turned poisonous again I
did not know. Perhaps it was the pressure of the approaching
guests, their judgement of me. He walked around switching on
the room's plug-in radiators, putting fresh candles very straight
into the candlesticks, brushing invisible fluff off the napkins. If I
would not admit the truth of my past, he would rather we didn't
speak at all. He had held a picture in his mind of how this day
would be – the leisurely breakfast, our cooking for the engagement
party, his consoling and supporting me over the mysterious
correspondence – and I'd not lived up to it. Even my drawing
breath now seemed to irritate him. I had become too familiar, as
though we'd been long married already.

'You must have really provoked that man to get him into this
state.'

I could see a sheet of paper on the sideboard, as if he'd just set
it down after rereading. 'But you think *he* was abusing *me*.'

'That doesn't stop me wondering how the hell you let him.
Some freak who can barely even spell.'

A freak like you? I thought.

'And please don't start going on about the letters with the
guests.'

'Why would I?'

He was rearranging the cutlery, making every knife and fork,
every dessert spoon and fork, exactly symmetrical. 'I mean, some

191

of my friends know the history of our relationship, but this correspondence is a private matter.'

'You said you hadn't told anybody.'

A gruff sigh. 'After the letters began coming I needed counsel.'

Feeling myself start to sway, I reached for the back of a chair. The air around us tasted stale again. My face was hot and stinging. How infinitely and exquisitely embarrassing. People other than Alexander now believed I was a hooker. And my fantasy – in a sense, the contents of my mind – had been made public.

I spoke just to hold on. 'Why don't we call the police?'

'Don't be an idiot.'

'Isn't this a crime?'

'How, exactly?'

'Slander comes to mind —'

Alexander snickered. 'You want me to call the police, and say, "Help! Until recently my fiancée was a prostitute, and now one of her clients is writing dirty letters to us"?'

'No, I'll call the police and say, "This *abuser*, this kerb-crawler, is holding me against my will!"'

'If you like.' He took the accusation calmly, but pushed the chair I'd been clasping hard under the table, straightening it. 'The rest of the district, those who don't already know your résumé, would certainly find out about it quickly.'

I saw a chance. 'You're ashamed of me.'

'No, I'm not.'

'If you're so ashamed why not just let me go?'

'But I'm not ashamed.' Alexander returned to full patrician mode. 'I've simply realised we will need to keep our life very private.'

'So you won't be defending my honour?'

'How can I?' His expression was free of all affection. 'The nutcase who wrote these letters could be anyone. What do you want me to do, open the White Pages?'

I knew then that I must never be let out. In his latest plan I would not leave this house, for if we were walking down the street of a nearby town someone might recognise me. In his imagination, any man he saw even fleetingly in a shop or restaurant window, anyone he met at a party or a cattle sale, could once have paid me for sex. *We won't go anywhere together,* I thought I heard him say, although his lips were not moving. *With you as my wife there will be nowhere I can take you.*

'Then for God's sake,' I asked, quietly, 'why marry a whore like me?'

He picked up the letter and folded it inside his pocket. 'Because I love you.'

PART THREE

I

I knew before now. That our game had gone too far.

This was the moment I realised: Alexander and I met outside an apartment for sale in Toorak, a supposedly exclusive Melbourne suburb. I greeted him professionally and let us both into the building's foyer. We rode the lift to the right floor and found the right door. Inside he handed me the usual envelope of money and I was already recalculating my debt as I took off my jacket, looking around the room to refresh my memory about an incident that had never happened. The owners had moved overseas, but to make the place desirable each room was full of rented furniture. Décor at the height of fashion, say, seven years ago – mainstream versions of 1960s space-age design, which invited sex that was clinical and stylised – the kind that people think they ought to have.

I began a story along these stark lines, and soon Alexander had pushed aside a hired tulip table to kneel in front of me as I perched on a hired armchair. My legs around his shoulders, I was close to losing myself; shutting my eyes, trying to disappear, I heard a knock on the door.

We both stopped still.

There had been close calls before. Once we'd been about to start when we heard a key turn in a lock. I'd scrambled to put my clothes back on, just as a cleaner bustled in carrying his strap-on vacuum. With my knickers now in Alexander's coat pocket I'd negotiated with the man to call back when the inspection was over. Then I'd returned to the room in which Alexander was waiting, only to find him standing in his suit barefoot. At the time I'd thought he was too nervous to finish dressing. But when I put my hand under his shirt to still his heartbeat, I found it perfectly calm.

Now the knocking began again – the quake of the timber panels and the metal safety chain rattling.

Alexander leaned over me, deeper inside me.

Unable, really, to move, I did not know if I should call out that this was a bad time. I didn't know if by not calling out, whoever it was on the other side of the door would think no one was home, and take a key from his pocket and open it. I did not know who had spare keys. Could my uncle? Had he seen the office car parked out the front and, as my phone was switched off, stopped to give me a message? I did not know if it was a friend of the owners checking the place was tidy. Or someone from downstairs who, hearing the noise above, wondered what was going on.

'Who is it?' Alexander didn't lower his voice.

Shaking my head, I mouthed, 'I've no idea.' The knocking sounded angry. It was as though this person knew what we were doing.

'Is it another client, early?'

'Be quiet.'

'Someone who couldn't wait?'

He was staring into my eyes, aroused by my panic. Did I wonder then if he was mad?

'I want you to open the door.'

'Please . . . be quiet.' I tried to prise his hands off my skin without making more noise.

'Go and open the door. Open it and let him see you are busy.'

Cautious Alexander was asking me to do this? I'd understood that the longer our trysting went on, the more likely it was to end in disaster. What I hadn't registered was that some part of Alexander thrilled to the idea of being found out. He actually wanted people to know.

Eventually the knocking had stopped, and by the time it did I'd decided our game was over. I'd leave Australia. It was my only choice. I could think of no other way to end this.

I was sitting at the white dressing table, replaying this episode as I combed my hair. I put down the comb and picked up a lipstick. I drew a mouth. I took a pencil and gave myself eyes, and with a brush, cheekbones, making a mask behind which I could hide. When I'd received his invitation here, I was caught between wanting to push this thing – and my earnings – as far as I could and the desire to be done with it.

Was there an easy way to put him off? I was always on the verge of confessing the truth, that a large part of me wasn't even very interested in sex, resented it in fact, and that this part actually found it mortifyingly teenage to be caught all day on a rat-wheel of lust, perpetually fussing over one or another moist, swollen private bit. Being on heat was like seeing the world through magic glasses; there was always another sexual dimension, each one more strenuous and absurd than the last. 'To be honest,' I'd tell him, 'I could happily do without the whole thing. You want to know who I am? That's it.'

Smoothing my dress, I left the bedroom, pulling closed the door.

I walked slowly down the grand staircase, listening for the humming of pleasantries in the rooms below, my hand on the carved wooden balustrade with one invalid finger, the ring fixed tight.

In the drawing room, Alexander sat with his back to the fire. He'd switched on various lamps, and the soft light made the furniture's upholstery appear less frayed, the birds in their glass case soothing shadows.

'You look beautiful,' he said.

An open bottle of champagne waited by a tray of six flutes.

I sat and took the glass he handed me. 'Your guests are late.'

'They'll be here soon.'

'What's that sound?'

'Curlews.'

'At night?'

'Yes.'

The calls came spinning through the pitch black and stayed in the air. Alexander did not speak further and neither did I.

I was waiting to see who he'd invited – and then, after a while, to see if he had actually invited anyone. He was waiting, I supposed, for me to crack. Twenty minutes, then half an hour went by. The bottle of champagne was drained without fanfare.

'No one's coming, are they?' I said finally.

Arranging his blazer cuffs, smoothing beige trousers: 'They will.'

'It's just going to be you and me.' I shook my head in disbelief. 'Who did you imagine we were waiting for, Alexander?'

'I am waiting for some friends of mine.'

'Who are they?'

'People I know,' he said plainly.

'What do these people do?'

'When you meet them, you can ask.' His smile suggested I should be quiet.

'Have they rung to say they're delayed?'

He began opening another bottle. 'No.'

I listened to the clock marking time. I'd banked on the arrival of four people – one of whom, surely, would help me. But with each minute I grew more desperate. I thought again of the knocking at that apartment.

Afterwards, I'd found an envelope stuck under the door, marked TO THE OCCUPIER – a bill perhaps, although seeing it waiting there I'd imagined it was the harshest possible rebuke for having sullied other people's homes. And even through this guilt, I still couldn't shake the feeling that Alexander was trying to find the limit to which he could push me. Did he have it in him to arrange for someone to come and knock? To hire an actor to pretend that he knew me?

'Are you expecting my ex-clients?' I now burst out. 'Is that who the table is set for?'

'Would you like that, Liese?' he asked quickly, eyes alert. 'What do you think we'd all talk about?'

'Your mothers, probably.'

'Really, is that right?' He nodded as though the guess were reasonable. 'That reminds me, I've found something I want to show you.' Putting down his glass, Alexander walked to the bureau and produced an old leather photo album. Undoing a copper clasp, he held it out to me as a teacher would a storybook. There was a portrait of a woman in white, costumed as if for a coronation, the dress's train spread before her and a bouquet of roses cascading to the floor.

My stomach knotted: obviously this was his mother. She was fair-haired, fair-faced, and gazing at the photographer with an expression of invitation much too liberal for one's wedding day. Anyone seeing that look would have expected this marriage to have problems.

'What do you think of the dress?' Alexander asked.

'The dress is very nice.'

'I agree.' He paused. 'Actually, I imagine it's packed away somewhere in the house.'

'Shall we try to find it?' It would be a chance to get him out of the room – this time I would grab a coat and run.

'I'll have to think about where it might be.' Stalling, Alexander bit his lip and took in the photograph once more. 'She was so lovely, so kind . . . Would the other men say similar things about their mothers?'

'I really couldn't tell you.'

'But what's your professional opinion? You said yourself you've had to talk to a lot of men about their families —'

The dogs began to bark and howl, followed by the sound of a car's wheels on the gravel. An engine was turned off. A door slammed. Footsteps – footsteps outside the house. In the dark this person approached the front door, then stopped, coughing. Both of us sat braced. The guest started rapping on the door's brass knocker.

'Oh, it's you,' I heard Alexander mutter when he answered it.

'Who were you expecting?' a woman replied.

He didn't say.

'Are you going to invite me in?'

Walking into the room, this thin, flat-chested woman looked familiar in some way I couldn't place. Long, blondish hair was clipped in chunks at the back of her head, crimson lipstick streaked her pale face; she was attractive, and had been very attractive, but her face showed the signs of someone who, having tried, had at last given in. She was dressed in a vintage burgundy pantsuit, which was made for someone shorter, more buxom, more flamboyant. Over this she'd incongruously thrown a khaki padded vest, bulky as a life jacket.

'This is Liese.'

I was smiling dumbly.

His hands on his hips, Alexander added rebelliously, 'Liese is a close friend of mine.'

'That's very nice,' the woman said.

'Actually, we're engaged.'

She laughed, a high uneven sound. Glancing at us both, one then the other. 'Brilliant.' She clicked her tongue. 'How brilliant.'

Was she Alexander's wife, or his ex-wife, or his ex-fiancée? Her outfit could have been from the wardrobe upstairs.

Picking up the champagne bottle she poured herself a generous glass, and still amused by something – perhaps me in a white dress, given what she'd heard – held it up in ironic tribute. 'You'll have to marry at St Johns. Have you been there, Liese?' She opened a corner cabinet, found an ashtray and lit a cigarette in jerky, fluttering movements. 'It's the local church. Alex's great-great-grandfather donated the stained-glass windows – some of the finest Victorian glass in this country.'

I was mute, still thinking, Surely this woman – whoever she is – can help me.

'It will be their wedding of the year!'

'Liese,' Alexander said sharply, 'would you mind giving us a moment?'

As I moved towards the hall, with plans to go upstairs and get my money, the woman sniggered.

'You really know how to pick them, don't you?'

'What do you actually want?' Alexander tried not to shout.

'I need to collect some things.'

'So get them. Just go and bloody get them.' Alexander peered out the window at the driveway.

The dogs resumed their maniacal noise: another car was on the gravel. As Alexander went to greet the new arrivals, the woman put down her drink. 'Excuse me,' she said dismissively, and shortly I heard her running up the stairs.

A middle-aged couple followed Alexander into the room. Dressed almost identically in pressed jeans and navy rollneck pullovers, they were the same height, the same austere build; even their hair was styled in standard-issue grey helmet cuts. The woman, however, wore a cross of beaten silver around her neck.

'Sorry to be late.' Already she was regarding me with curiosity. 'We rang continually but your phone must be out. The Barrett-Joneses tried calling too. Willow has her usual stomach problems – they send their apologies.'

Alexander turned to me, his eyes a cold blue. 'My love, the Reverend Wendy Smythe. Wendy is our local minister, and Graeme, her better half.'

'Congratulations.' Her tone was no-nonsense.

I opened my mouth but no words would come.

She nodded. 'It must be a lot for you to take in.'

With the arrival of the woman upstairs I'd gained my first witness – if she proved unreliable I now had two more to choose from. I took it my imprisonment was effectively over: you don't abduct someone with plans to release and hunt them down in the national park – because *yes*, that was where my mind had gone – then invite around a bunch of spectators.

Gazing now at my soon to be ex-fiancé I found myself affecting a kind of awestruck, moist-eyed simulacrum of love. My voice, softer and higher than usual, finally worked. 'Oh, Reverend, I feel I'm the luckiest girl alive!'

The minister positioned herself on an overstuffed gentleman's chair. 'Have you set a date?'

I felt myself flush as if on cue. 'No, it's all been so sudden.'

'When a committed bachelor finally finds Miss Right there's no time to waste.' Alexander passed the guests pâté and biscuits. Beckoning for me to sit next to him on the couch, he squashed my hand in his. 'If I had my way, we'd all be down at the church tomorrow morning. Liese is more cautious, but I'm hoping to persuade her to speed things up.' He was hiding unease with joviality. 'Wendy, what are you doing,' he mimed glancing at his watch, 'say, tomorrow afternoon?'

The minister turned to her husband, signalling he should laugh. The sound he made was nervous. Like a humble servant in a play, he had the habit of ducking his head whenever I met his gaze.

'Enough about us,' I said. 'Graeme, what do you do?'

It took a moment for him to register he'd been asked a question.

'He plays the guitar and sings for our elderly community,' Reverend Wendy explained.

'A troubadour!'

Graeme blushed. 'I try to keep the set upbeat and bright, that's all.'

As his wife detailed his musical programme, I nodded and smiled. I found it easy enough to play the chaste bride (especially when I saw how much the act was irritating my fiancé). My exit strategy solved, I could not resist fucking with him a little. He'd paid for a whore, not a prim bride-to-be. Mock gentility seemed appropriate – I held my champagne flute, a little finger flaring, and took delicate, lizard sips, smiling straight through his scowls to assess this situation. I had wanted to cry with gratitude upon seeing other people, but all the while the minister spoke I felt a new disquiet. She regarded me knowingly with two very seasoned eyes.

'Have you called your parents?' Reverend Wendy asked.

'Oh, they're over the moon!'

'And they're from Norfolk . . .' It was half a question.

'Yes.' I met her gaze even as I felt Alexander's.

'So you *are* still in contact with them?'

I hesitated: exactly what had the minister been told?

She spread pâté thinly on a biscuit. 'Will they mind you living so far away?'

'There's plenty of room here. After I've redecorated, just knocked down a few walls and lightened the place up,' I coughed, 'I'd adore it if Mum and Dad could spend part of the year with us. No, Alexander's teasing you, I can hardly wait!'

'Very well.' The minister inhaled deeply, finishing the hors-d'oeuvre. 'If you feel you're ready, truly ready,' swallowing again, 'I will try to move at your speed . . .' She waited for one of us to back out. 'Okay, I've put together a list of questions, twenty-five questions, which you might want to consider.'

Graeme retrieved his wife's old leather satchel, and from it took two photocopied sheets, handing one to Alexander and one to me.

'THE BIG TWENTY-FIVE'

PRE-MARITAL COUNSELLING QUESTIONS

The minister remained grave. 'I'm afraid I never just marry couples without fulfilling my pastoral duties.'

'We understand —' I began.

'But we'd like to start now,' Alexander cut in.

'Well, usually I do one or two sessions before the ceremony. Some of the questions will strike you as remedial. In fact, you can have a good laugh over them, but I hope they'll help us move on to the serious stuff, and address any niggling doubts about,' she paused, 'about compatibility.' A biscuit crumb was squatting in the downturned corner of her mouth. 'We'll then get together – nothing formal, of course, just with a cup of tea – and talk about your thoughts, impressions, the difficult spots you might have encountered.'

I glanced down at the questions.

1 Why do you want to marry?
2 Why do you want to marry me?
3 What values do we share?
4 Do you plan to attend church after our marriage?
5 What is your image of God?

The curlews called from outside. My image of God – and the proof of his existence – would be this house shrinking in the rear-view mirror as I sped away.

6 Is it important to know one another's physical/ mental health history?
7 Do you have a criminal record?
8 Have you ever hit anyone?

From out in the hallway came a loud clanging – something heavy had fallen. The minister glanced at Alexander in alarm.

13 What are your expectations of our sexual relationship?
14 Are we comfortable discussing our sexual likes and dislikes together?
15 Are we prepared to forsake all others?
16 Do you expect or want me to change?

The blonde woman's footsteps echoed on the hall tiles, along with her expletives.

25 Can we both forgive?

Walking back into the room, she stuffed a metallic object into a soft black travel bag.

'Reverend Wendy, Graeme,' Alexander had stiffened, 'obviously you know my sister, Annabel.'

Annabel's bag bulged with chattels that, judging by how tenderly she put it down to greet the guests, must have been valuable. Her arms were outstretched with that posh mix of hauteur and intimacy which made it impossible to tell if she loved or despised them. The minister patted her back in a manner suggesting a history of forbearance.

'Thank you,' Annabel said, turning to her brother. Her accent, like his, had that fruity, gentrified strain. 'We'd be delighted to stay for dinner – Lachie's out in the car, I'll go and get him.'

Exiting, she slammed the front door hard behind her.

I smiled at Alexander but he was staring at the floor.

Outside Annabel was yelling, and these yells were matched by another's. At last she re-entered with gangly, eczema-ridden Lachie slouching in after her. Shrunken and confused by long exposure to the embarrassment of his mother, he greeted his uncle awkwardly, and answered the minister's predictable questions in monosyllables slurred through the stud on his tongue.

Would the last hours in this house be spent enduring a family dinner? With me now zoning out, fixing on the particles of dust floating on the surface of the champagne, and the carpet's thousand knots blurred through the bottom of the glass? The siblings' skirmishes made my former terror seem so foolish.

'Darling? My love?'

I realised Alexander was talking to me.

'Will you show our guests to the table?'

In candlelight the dining room felt cave-like. Even with the various portable heaters switched on the room was still cross-hatched with draughts. On the table, my outsize floral arrangement was central.

His sister stood at the door, holding the ashtray. 'Where do you want us?'

'Annabel, will you sit to Alexander's right, and Reverend Wendy to his left. Graeme and Lachie, if you'll come next to me.' Impersonating the ideal fiancée, I was all the while thinking, This is the moment to say something, with him in the kitchen this is the moment to act. As the guests arranged themselves around the table, my half-open mouth was trying to form the right words:

Please, you have to help me. He's been holding me captive . . . But had Alexander been holding me captive? I could now no longer tell. One moment he seemed close enough to reasonable, restoring an orchard, caring for his animals in need, the next a madman, who'd written a guide on ways to molest me.

The clock in the hallway struck nine o'clock – I started, and caught my stricken face reflected in the glass of the French doors. Past this, the moon was in a mean phase.

'Well, you're a brave woman.' It was his sister.

'How is that?'

'We just never expected Alexander to marry. He has rather enjoyed his freedom, that's all.' She was staring down, her scratched fingers rearranging the cutlery. 'Whenever he's seemed close to walking down the aisle . . . we don't know, something's always happened.'

'What sort of thing?'

She gave a little shrug. 'How did you meet?'

All of them, even the teenager, seemed to collectively resist one huge smirk as they pictured him winding down his car window on a dark street corner.

'I work in real estate,' I said defensively. 'Alexander is interested in a property investment.'

'Well, *you've* certainly found a nice property here.' Graeme tried for conviviality before his wife shot him a look.

'Oh yes, he's rich now he's sending his sheep to the Middle East.' Annabel leaned across the table and adjusted her son's knife and fork too. 'If the animals survive the journey – no, that's not fair,' she conceded, 'I hear the boats are wonderful these days, it's when they arrive that their throats are cut.'

Alexander re-entered the room, using oven mitts to carry a large silver tray.

'I was telling Liese about your live exports.'

'Lachlan, move those flowers, will you?' With a fixed grin, he waited as his nephew cleared a space for him to place the tray. Upon it was the great gleaming bird surrounded by its mound of vegetables. 'Yes, invest in Australian agriculture, you can't go wrong.'

'And how the animals die very painful deaths.'

Alexander turned to the minister. 'Reverend Wendy, would you mind saying grace?'

'Oh, certainly.' Layering her chin she stared down at a monogrammed plate. 'Thank you, our Lord, for bringing us together to celebrate this occasion with our good friends, Liese and Alexander – and his family.'

Annabel pushed back her chair, clasping her cigarette packet.

'Thank you for your wisdom and grace in helping Liese and Alexander to meet each other,' the minister continued, 'for giving Liese her career in real estate, and Alexander the need for . . . shelter. Thank you, Lord, for showing them your love through their love for one another . . .'

My head lowered, I tried to ignore the diamond ring putting on its little light show. Glancing around the table, I wondered who I should ask for a lift. His sister may have hated him, but blood was thicker than water, I reasoned, turning to the minister and Graeme. They were people of God – surely their consciences would be good for a ride into town. And yet I could not be sure what Alexander had told them about me. About the letters.

'May this couple always find haven in each other.' Reverend Wendy was raising her head. 'And may they know they enjoy our friendship and support in their union. Amen.'

'Amen,' mouthed her husband.

Standing, Alexander sharpened a bone-handled carving knife and started dividing up the bird.

I addressed the minister: 'Do you think Jesus loved Mary Magdalene because she was a prostitute, or despite that fact?'

'Honestly,' Alexander spat, 'what sort of conversation is that?'

'No, no, I don't mind.' Reverend Wendy cleared her throat. Her speed in answering suggested she'd been considering the issue. 'Luke 7 does seem to refer to her as blemished. I mean,' she added, 'by the standards of the day. *And, behold, a woman in the city, which was a sinner.* In the Apocrypha, however, Mary Magdalene is depicted as one of Jesus's most learned and beloved supporters, so,' the minister tilted her head from side to side, mimicking scales, 'I tend to think the patriarchy's having another free kick, and now Hollywood has glamorised the idea.'

'Wendy has done a lot of counselling,' Graeme explained, 'around St Kilda, which – Liese may or may not know – is Melbourne's red-light district.'

'She's discreet, of course,' Annabel vouched, a touch ambiguously; she lit a cigarette.

'Some sex workers who've sought help turn their lives right around.' Reverend Wendy's nod was meaningful. 'Girls – very, very young sometimes, and in the grip of dreadful heroin addictions.'

'*Junkies?*' Alexander used the word like it might bite. He was irritated, even offended. 'If we have to talk about this, the point is that the woman was in some way fallen and Jesus forgave her.' He was looking around the table for back-up. 'He forgave her. It's a story about tolerance.'

'It might not be about *him* forgiving *her*!' I was practically shouting. 'He should have forgiven those who spread lies about her, all the hypocrites and bigots who can't stop themselves judging!'

For a while no one spoke.

Annabel blew smoke towards the ceiling.

'That's definitely not duck,' Graeme said eventually.

'Nor goose,' added Reverend Wendy, taking a bite, rolling it in her mouth. 'This is almost fishy.'

We stared at our plates, silent.

'Well?' Alexander had the air of a man with the punchline.

Raising the dark meat to my lips, my mouth would not open. 'It's swan,' I realised aloud. The one I'd seen on our picnic?

'So wait! Like you went out and shot this bird?' Gazing out from a low fringe, Alexander's nephew was suddenly keen-eyed.

'Basically, yes.'

'And did you get it by stealth kind of thing, using a scope?'

Lachlan's mother stubbed out her cigarette on the side of her plate. 'He probably wrung its neck.'

'No, that wouldn't be sportsmanlike,' Alexander answered. 'The bird should always be in flight.'

'What size cartridge?'

'Size four.' He coughed. 'I used your grandfather's old Browning.'

'And it took one shot?'

'It's far more difficult, Lachlan, to shoot a swan than, say, a duck.' Alexander bit his lip. 'They're all neck, and a size-four cartridge has fewer pellets. Anyway, the dogs found where the bird landed and it was extremely aggressive; it scared the hell out of them. No, I needed two shots.'

Bile rose in my throat as I thought of the creature I'd watched gliding over the lake . . . Now the image would fix in my head of the dogs finding the bird. And the bird knowing it was going to die, hissing as it tried to fight back, flaring its wings, thrashing, wild-eyed, desperate.

Rising woozily to my feet, I asked, 'How could you?'

The others stopped, recoiling.

'How could you do this?'

Alexander looked like a child reprimanded in public – resentful, churlish – but also slyly pleased to see me so unhinged. 'Liese, sit down.'

'No, I will not.'

'Sit down.'

'Don't ever tell me what to do!'

'Fine. Stand there screaming in front of our guests.' He forked the bird's meat up to his mouth.

As I headed to the door, the minister made a move to follow me, but he raised his hand. 'Don't worry,' I heard him say, 'she's just in a mood. I thought she liked swans.'

My heels were out of time on the tiled floor.

Walking past the staircase, I turned down the corridor to the rear of the house. There was a sour, sickening, *alive* taste in my mouth. I could smell feathers on my breath, feel them on my tongue.

My shoulder was hard against the back door, and when it opened I fell outside, gasping for real air. A lemon tree stood sentry and I was next to it, doubled over, trying to vomit, while coughing up nothing. Had he done this after he'd seen how the bird thrilled me? My lungs burned with the night's chill; tears streamed down my face. *I hate you. I hate you completely. I would rather die than ever marry you.* That some part of me, some infinitesimal feminine part, had even considered this a possibility added to the nausea. Walking around in small circles of disgust, I cried and heaved in the dark. After eating little for the past two days I had fallen on the meat, and each piece I'd swallowed now felt like acid in my gut.

A dog growled out a long low note of suspicion.

I stopped.

Remember the children's game where one player turns and the other players, right behind her, mimic statues? There was no one else behind me but the trees were playing that game, acting still, a fake sort of still, while something fluttered in the highest branches. I could hear these branches moving in the wind, but glancing up, all I saw were out-of-focus stars. The air's bite, at first welcome and purifying, now made the shiver in the small of my back turn chronic.

Slowly I started walking around the house's perimeter, my hand pressed against the cold bluestone walls. The rear of this place was like the back of a stage set. There were pipes and exposed wiring and small dark windows.

I passed a corner and stepped through rectangles of light coming from the dining room's glass doors onto the veranda.

'I stared in at the room, all lit up with money and perversion. Alexander and his guests were sitting around the table, talking amongst themselves as though nothing had happened.

That's my engagement party, I thought.

I was hurt: this sick part of me had almost enjoyed playing the bride-to-be. It was akin to telling oneself an old, old fairytale that included bridesmaids carrying posies of wildflowers, a veil blowing in the breeze, confetti and rose petals raining down . . . How could I have known that all the soothing stories of girlhood would spring up like so many seeds waiting for a fire to germinate them?

Even now, I could half picture putting tables under the trees – covering them in white cloths, with all the table settings white too, but for place cards in an Edwardian-style font. We could find a caterer who specialised in slow food. There would be a wedding cake frosted with ivory icing and sugar flowers – gardenias, roses, lily of the valley – and I'd arrange candles throughout the trees, hanging them from branches with white satin ribbon . . .

I turned, disgusted again, and with the light from the dining room made out in the darkness the shape of a car – a station wagon. Across the gravel I walked towards it. I could just read the insignia stencilled on the side, 'Colquhoun's Roses of Distinction', circling the image of a bud. As I opened the door it made an aching noise, as though bending the wrong way: low bucket seats with ripped upholstery, the overwhelming smell of manure, of blood and bone. I immediately shut the door, gagging.

Some way down the driveway I spied another car, a silver sedan. Shaking now, I went to it.

If I just hid here on the back seat, if I just lay down and waited, then the minister and Graeme would have to take me away from this place. I'd demand they drive me to a hospital, or a police station, and I'd wait there until a bus came travelling to Melbourne.

The car had central locking and when I pressed down one lock every door clicked. Leaning my head against the headrest, I swallowed hard. So close to safety, I needed it immediately. A deodoriser hung from the rear-view mirror, and next to me on the seat there was a box of tissues, a safety kit, the Bible – I took hold of it.

On school excursions we'd visit Norwich Cathedral and wheel a mirror-topped trolley over the vaulted floors to look at the wooden carvings on the ceilings. All the stories, from the Fall of Man to the Resurrection of Jesus, blended together: there was Noah on his ark surrounded by animals; a wounded Doubting Thomas; the Pharaoh drowning in the Red Sea with his followers' naïve faces only just bobbing out of the water; Adam and Eve smooth and naked, kneeling under a tree of golden apples, the serpent waiting . . .

If Alexander *had* written the letters I could truly say that in some strange way he knew me. I'd told him true things and he'd extrapolated. I'd told him false things but parts of his letters were still true. That was what was unnerving: amongst the madness there was insight.

My own desire could make me feel obscene. It could make me feel sluttish and out of control. And as the letters pointed out, the money seemed a way to manage this. It gave my vast and clumsy longings a neater shape, a strategic purpose. This was functional shame. But, of course, shame can only be resized like this for so long before it bursts out. Shame had been built into the very act of taking his money; it washed over me each time I was paid, brief but extra potent. It was the deeper for being in someone else's house. The sex itself drove the feeling back for a while but I suppose doing ever wilder things to avoid shame was bound to bring more of it.

Reading the letters had taken me inside my own head. I recognised all the murky, half-hidden parts – the feeling of being indecently different, and the old yearning to be someone else. On those cathedral excursions the other children are playing and I am the big girl who lurks at the side, watching. Standing under the great limestone arches is like being in the shell *and* the wave. And a switch turns on and I find I can sleepwalk through this day while in my alternative, secret world magic possibilities roll out before me . . . I'd left home and remade myself as best I could – but now, sitting in a stranger's car, there was horror in these layers of invention. The letters made me feel deeply that I had no secrets left. Even their lies seemed to show me for who I really was. Did getting close to another always mean discovering you were a fraud?

A flash of silver – dangling in the ignition, the car keys were reflecting the moonlight. Crawling straight over to the driver's seat, I sat and laughed. So this was how it ended: I would go howling into the dark night! I'd worry about changing my life later. For now, adjusting the car seat, I turned the key in the ignition and I was blazing with victory! I pressed down on the accelerator and the engine roared – nothing happened. The car was manual. I did not know how to drive a manual. I pushed the gearstick and heard crunching. When I pushed it harder, it was worse.

'Liese!' Alexander's voice, calling from a distance.

I got out of the car and picked a rock up off the ground.

'Liese!' Alexander again, then other voices, the guests': 'Lee-ease!'

Dogs were barking. Someone had a torch.

Dropping the rock, I charted my path through the darkness towards the back of the house. Each step was over hard earth, but listening to the guests' calls felt dreamlike. Had this happened before? And if so, to whom? Whose déjà vu was I experiencing?

Lachlan was standing by the back door, smoking.

I grabbed his slender arm. 'Do you know how to drive a manual?'

Already he was stubbing out the cigarette, coughing. 'Yeah.'

'I'll give you a thousand dollars if you get me to a railway station.'

'Jesus!' He sounded tempted, but he hesitated.

'I'll make it worth your while,' I found myself saying. '*Really* worth it.'

I moved closer to him. My hand drifted from his arm to his chest. Even in the dark I could tell he was trembling.

His voice was higher now. 'Let me ask Mum to borrow the keys.'

'No need.' I tried for an impression of calm. 'Reverend Wendy's car has the keys in it.'

Lachlan was bending down, burying his cigarette butt and covering its grave in another layer of soil. 'Umm, I don't actually have my licence.'

I turned and walked through the back door. This nightmare

was such a perfect fit that I didn't know how to step out of it, how to shake it off my back. In Alexander's study, I checked to see if he had replaced the letters. I wanted each one. I needed to take them with me when I left as evidence. Evidence of how he'd tapped into the part of my brain that ran a hate campaign against me. Opening one drawer of his desk after another, I pulled out the contents and dumped all of it on the floor. The letters were gone.

Out the window I could hear Alexander and the others still calling my name.

I crept from the study down the hallway and ran up the stairs to the pink bedroom. I'd planned to take the envelope of money and stash it somewhere before leaving. (If nothing else, it could pay for therapy.) But staring at the notes I now felt myself shudder. For all these months his cash had seemed to have magical properties, to be some elixir that could clear my debts and every other ill. It was only cash, though. Rectangles of plastic in gaudy colours. Didn't Freud compare it to excrement?

The door swung open.

The minister: her features at first mirroring my fright, before bright eyes betrayed a stern satisfaction.

'Found her!' she called out. 'We'll be back down in a minute!' Reverend Wendy shut the door carefully so as not to startle her prey.

I spoke first: 'Help me!'

'Of course.'

'I am not who he thinks I am,' I urged through clenched teeth. 'Who you think I am.'

Reverend Wendy composed her face as if she understood

exactly. 'My dear, let me say this: a lot of girls these days have a past.'

'What's that supposed to mean?' In my right hand I held the envelope of cash tightly to my hip.

The minister half shrugged, uncomfortable at the need to spell it out.

'Look, I am not a sex worker, okay?'

'No, no.' She glanced at the envelope as I moved it further behind my back. 'No one's saying you are, dear, but early in a partnership carnal relations are central to men's self-identity. Later, you know, with children, et cetera, everyone's tired . . .'

I stared at her in disbelief. 'Did you see what he did to the swan?'

'You mustn't be so sensitive,' she said harshly.

'He killed it as a warning. He did it to frighten me!'

'Not at all.' The minister was straining to appear sympathetic. 'Swans have been discreetly culled around here for decades.' Visibly she shifted to a lower gear, treating me as though I'd just thrown a tantrum. 'Alexander lives off the land, or that's his plan. He's a gourmand who strives to use totally local ingredients, and I personally feel it should be commended.'

'Reverend, you don't seem to understand – I am *trapped* here.'

She regarded me without comprehending.

My God, I thought, was it possible this woman had a crush on him?

'He won't let me go, he won't let me leave.'

'Well, he's smitten.' A brisk smile.

'No.' I now spat each word. '*I am physically trapped.*'

'You went outside before, Liese.' Unimpressed, she was patting herself, searching for her glasses, which were the plainest, wire-rimmed frames one could buy. Having dealt with junkies and other down-and-outs, she had no time for this self-indulgence. 'On the surface marriage makes us feel under another's control, but truly it offers a kind of liberation. For some it can also be a chance to start afresh,' she added pointedly. 'I suppose I was nervous too before I was married. It's only natural.'

Reverend Wendy peered at the row of porcelain ponies lined up along the mantelpiece. 'Goodness,' she said, 'this must have been Annabel's room.'

I placed the money back in the suitcase, making no attempt to hide what I was doing.

Tactfully, the minister kept inspecting the figurines. 'Anyway, your fiancé is about to make a speech. You'd better come back.'

Don't they say sociopaths can act in minute detail the part they wish to play? Their mimicry is so precise that in the end it's difficult to be sure whether it *is* an act. From a particular angle, the man standing by the dining table with his hand upon my shoulder was still attractive, and even, at a stretch, charming. If one believed his speech he appeared the model fiancé and his devotion to me was, as the minister assumed, very moving. If one wasn't sure whether to believe him – as I was not – it was terrifying.

I stared at the mahogany tabletop: the plates had been cleared, the swan's carcass moved to a sideboard. Alexander's hand pressed harder into my flesh.

'What really is romantic love?' he asked, turning philosophical. 'Is it a biological imperative? A spiritual state? A form of delusion? Man may have asked himself these questions for millennia, but until recently, I confess, I'd never bothered.

'The idea of "true" love was, I'd always believed, just a fairy story to help people avoid facing how utterly alone we are. We are alone,' he said straightening. 'We are alone – and people, generally, live alienated from nature. Then they fixate on finding the perfect other human half, and attach a lot of mystical qualities to the pursuit.' He gave a bemused sigh. 'These people are unable to bear that really we are animals with the same basic needs and desires as those standing with four legs outside in the paddocks.

'So, I have been . . .' Pausing, Alexander leaned down and put his fingers underneath my chin, tilting my face to his. A thin line of sweat glistened on his forehead, the candlelight shading then dazzling his features. 'I have been a bachelor for a long time now, and I've always sidled away from the girls who caught the bouquet. However, despite what's been a very successful year for the farm,' Alexander was staring into my eyes, 'many nights I returned to this house knowing something profound was missing. Always one glass and plate and knife and fork drying by the sink, and no one to share one's thoughts with. Always too many rooms feeling emptier each year.

'Now,' he ducked his head, shyly, curls spilling over his forehead, 'growing up in this house was not always pleasant. Reverend, I know Annabel's spoken with you about this, as have I. It wasn't easy . . . Nevertheless, I have strong memories of my dear mum almost begging me to find a nice girl and settle down.'

At the mention of her mother, Annabel made a noise like something was burning in her throat. The minister filled her empty wineglass with water.

'Not – and let's be frank – not that I always felt Mum would have approved of the girls I did bring home . . .' He paused for laughter. '"And where," I asked her in my head, "do you think I'll meet this nice girl?" "Go to Melbourne," I heard her advise, "take a house for the season and have a good time." So I drove down to the city and on the way made an appointment to look for a *pied-à-terre*. And who'd have thought she would be right? From the moment I met Liese, I displayed all the symptoms of an animal in love. For yes,' he grinned, 'in mating season all species behave differently, even experiencing what could be called "the blues". When it seemed Liese returned my feelings, my heart soared; when I wasn't so certain, I'd drive back here to drag myself around for days. *Come to me in my dreams, and then/By day I shall be well again!*'

With each sweet word I felt the room closing in on me. Locked into his story now, I watched his mouth move, those full lips wet with satisfaction, and I wondered whether for all these months I too had been caught in his gun-sight while he decided the best time to bring me down.

'Liese, you are my chance to be well again, my chance at happiness,' Alexander said, his glance adding, If you understand you are the object meant to guarantee my contentment, you will be all right. He smoothed his hands against his trousers. 'Please raise your glasses, ladies and gentlemen, and join me in toasting my new life and bride-to-be.'

His cough told the guests they ought to stand.

Numbly I joined them, and taking my shoulders Alexander pulled me towards him, kissing me on the mouth: a kiss like he needed resuscitation. With it, I tasted the swan, and I was suddenly woken and filled with horror. Was I being kissed by a man deeply in love with me, or by a devil doing a perfect imitation of a man deeply in love with me?

His sister was the only one still seated. 'You're just like he was.'

The minister and Graeme paused, their champagne glasses frozen in the air.

'Even the way you speak, the things you say.'

'Not now, Annabel.'

'Dad would have liked nothing more than to lock her away for good, get her out of his sight. He'd have been proud of how well you managed it.'

Alexander turned to his sister. 'Did *you* want to care for her after the crash?'

'Didn't she . . .?' I started clumsily. 'I thought your mother had died?'

'That's what he told you?'

'Well, she is dead now, Annabel.'

'And to think you meant the world to her! When you were a child you'd cry if she went out, and wait on the stairs until she got back.' Annabel's large eyes, rimmed with tears, settled on her own son, who had clearly heard all this before. 'But Lachlan, after Grandpa died, your grandma had to live with her injuries for many, many painful years, and your uncle moved her out of here and put her in what was ironically called a *home* —'

'She was well looked after.'

'Took her from her surroundings where she recognised everything, was comfortable, and put her with every village idiot —'

'I didn't see you round here volunteering to wipe up her messes.'

'Lachlan, before you ever do that to me, please kill me first!' She'd started crying, leaning her wet and red face against the table. In her mother's clothes she looked both very old and young.

'It's difficult,' the minister tried to intervene, 'when a parent becomes infirm —'

'Although then,' Annabel spat, 'your uncle could bring his little whores round here without anyone bothering him.'

Silence – even the night sounds from the garden cut out.

She turned to Alexander, mouth loose and twisting. 'You bring them in and then dump them however it best suits you.'

His features shifted into blankness. 'It's late. I think it might be time for you to go.'

'You need help, can't you see? You are not well, you need help!'

'Annabel, we don't have to do this.' He said it almost sadly. Moving to the door, he switched on the light.

The room was sulphuric. Everyone looked their worst. Even the furniture turned faded and dusty.

'And you.' Annabel reached for me, foundation streaking her cheeks. 'Can't you see he's sick? You should leave with us now. You should leave while you still have the chance!'

The minister and Graeme were on either side of her, trying

to coax her from the table. Lachlan, his mouth a thin line of resignation, picked up his mother's bag of pilfered objects and headed outside.

Annabel lurched past her minders and grabbed my hand. 'Come with me!'

Alexander stepped in to prise her off.

'Come on!'

The woman's raw, wet face was right in mine, chunks of her wild hair in my eyes, my mouth. We were now out in the hallway. No corner was left for my own hysteria. I would have to hide in hers.

'Come *on*.'

I looked from sister to brother.

'Yes, yes, I will,' I said, nodding. 'I will. I'll come with you.' Putting my hand to her arm I joined with her. The money was still upstairs but it no longer mattered. 'I'm coming, don't worry. I'll come.'

She was heading towards the doorway, calmer now she believed she was saving me. And I was calmer too, despite my saviour walking so unevenly that I was holding her up. I brushed her ribcage, and felt how starved she was. Graeme stepped in and took her other arm, and the three of us moved a little further along the patterned tiles, navigating the octagons and hexagons bursting underfoot in dusky blue and umber and beige. And we were closer to the door. Then her son returned and, shifting me out of the way, took his mother's free arm. The two of them led her outside.

The minister was standing in the doorway, the dark night behind her. 'Thank you,' she said, as if I'd just been playing along with Annabel and the trick to get her into the sedan. She nodded to Alexander. 'We'll take it from here. Graeme can come and collect her car in the morning.'

'I think I should still go with you,' I suggested firmly.

'Lachlan's got her tablets. There's no need.'

Alexander had put his hand tightly around my arm.

'But I *want* to leave with you.'

The minister glanced at him. 'There's no room in the car.'

'I'll squeeze in.' He was holding me the exact way I'd just held his sister. 'Please!'

Reverend Wendy cleared her throat and turned to walk down the stone steps. Past her the garden was a chessboard; between the trees were moonlit patches like chances.

'Liese, congratulations again,' she called over her shoulder. 'I think you are so lucky, and I look forward to talking over your marriage questions soon.'

And with that, Alexander closed the broad front door. I was screaming to those outside. The sound was echoing, but my fiancé ignored it as he started pulling me slowly up the stairs to the master bedroom.

II

There was only silence and the dripping tap's *to die, to die, to die.* On the vanity waited his new envelope. It was A4, a generic mustard colour available from any post office or stationery store in any part of the world, but it had not been posted. BY HAND was written like a sick joke in neat capitals on the top right-hand corner, and in the same script that usually addressed Alexander was substituted my own name:

Miss Liese Campbell
c/o 'Warrowill'
Marshdale
Victoria

I was sitting in the ensuite's bath in water so brown it seemed to have been pumped from deep underground. Neither of us moved to turn the tap tighter. I could barely move at all. Each part of my body felt tender and swollen.

Alexander stood by the mirrored cabinet, hunting through old and new beauty products. The room was so cold the mirror had turned opaque, and condensation rolled down the walls' mauve tiles. But even through the bath's mist, morning light from the window meant that if he cared to look he could see each part of me: breasts sloping, flesh folding around the midriff, the webbing of cellulite, the veins stretching under my skin.

In the dark the night before, he'd worked his fingers underneath my clothes, between skin and flesh. Then, not just his fingers, his fists, to get more leverage, his touch so rough it felt like he wore gloves, as if a hide protected him from any sensitivity to another. It had not bothered him that I was unresponsive, barely moving, barely breathing. And now this intercourse – or whatever our strange overnight battle had been – meant I felt him on my body, in my body, and it wiped out any will. Thoughts of surrendering came and they were sweet.

'Just try to relax,' Alexander said.

He selected a grimy-necked bottle of bath oil and knelt beside the bath on a matching mauve mat so as not to wet his good trousers. The sleeves of his shirt were rolled up, and leaning forward he poured the thick liquid onto my back, my shuddering back. He replaced the bottle's cap and started moving a flannel over my skin, rubbing very gently.

'Not enough,' he told himself, unscrewing the cap again and tipping more oil onto his palm, washing my arm, arranging me so his hand slipped under my armpit, touching the side of my breast.

'Relax,' he ordered again.

I did not move.

Taking my shoulders, Alexander positioned me so my neck was against the bath's rim. 'There, like that.' His face was very close. I could see the colour of his teeth and smell the night's drinking on his breath. His hands, muscular knots, wrung out the flannel in the brown water. He started on my legs and arse. He seemed to be feeling for where the muscle was, the bone and tendons, which parts were best and most tender – the prime cuts.

Keeping the flannel between my legs, his hand began to contract. 'You didn't tell me this person has been writing to you too.'

'This person has not been.'

'It's the first time? Is that what you're claiming?'

I wanted him to take his hand away. 'Yes.'

'So he has written this and delivered it all the way out here?' Alexander waited. 'And not even to the door, right inside the house and straight to my desk?' When I didn't answer he took the cloth from my sore skin, passing it to me. 'Perhaps you should clean yourself.'

Drying his hands, he picked up the envelope and, making a play at nonchalance, studied it. He was angrier than I had realised – or angry again, or angry still – his face gaunt and dark, like someone had sketched it in pencil then forgotten to erase the lines. He turned the envelope over, examining it, and the acting out of this – his ignorance as to its origins, his futile search for some clue – was almost camp. The visit from his sister must have brought too much reality, forcing him further into this game.

'How, Liese, do you figure this courier got in without starting up the dogs?'

Breathing very shallowly so the bathwater did not move:
'I couldn't tell you.'

'Could you have put it there when you looked through my
desk drawers?'

'No.'

'But you were in my study last night.' Exhaling he made a
hissing noise. 'I found papers all over the floor, the room was
ransacked.'

I shook my head, trying to keep the water calm.

It was true that after my failed escape in the car I had entered
his study. I'd wanted to take the letters as proof. Proof of what
he'd done to me. Alexander's refusal to acknowledge that they were
his creations made me think he wasn't so much lying as splitting.
It was Alexander who sat down at his desk but it was someone
else, a stranger, who started writing – and this stranger seemed to
know Alexander's fantasies better than he did. Each new dispatch
was a more dire self-provocation. Each revealed desires he could
evidently express no other way: I was to be just a catalogue of body
parts, serving or servicing some man's needs. What sane person
would dream about another becoming less than an animal, a lump
of meat, a *thing*?

'Are there signs anyone broke into the house?' I asked quietly.

'None.'

'What if it was one of the guests who left it?'

'I don't think so.'

'Well.' I was ready to give up. 'Perhaps it was a ghost.'

'Don't be sarcastic.'

'One of your ancestors.'

He said nothing.

'Your father, maybe?'

His father had often been absent and yet he'd never written to his son, not even a postcard, Alexander had said. As a boy, did he sometimes write to himself as if from his father? Did he still? The letters seemed to belong to a voice in Alexander's head, a voice with power over him. And I wondered if he would obey it.

He remained silent.

'Or are the letters from your mother?'

It seemed obvious enough, too obvious really: I was lying in her bath after all, surrounded by her effects; one set of makeup from before her accident, another for afterwards. If he felt guilty about turning his mother out, putting her in a home, was his remedy to keep me, the poor substitute, here and unable to leave? The letters were full of old-fashioned misogyny. The sort of thoughts a mother who does not want her son to marry might have, the thoughts a loyal son might imagine his mother would write to him anonymously.

'No, I don't think that's correct either.'

Then the letters must be from you, I wanted to say. But why?

At the beginning of this weekend Alexander had claimed, 'I just want to know who you are, who you really are.' Had he orchestrated all of this, each mad instalment, to see me behave in every possible way, to witness my whole range – and to prove how much of it he could control?

Both of us were staring at the envelope. That was the sick thing: despite my fear, my terror really, it *was* tempting to unseal it.

He passed it to me.

'I don't want to.'

'There isn't a choice.'

Slipping my fingernail underneath the edge, I pulled out the contents.

The first photograph was so out of focus it looked like the two figures – the man and the woman – were hovering in space, their outlines trembling. Where were they? There was something familiar about the room, I'll admit that, perhaps because the space was so generic. I studied it closely in case the dark parts of the image surrendered some secret: the shape of a vase, a corner of furniture. I was focusing on anything but the couple in the picture. The man – a stranger – and the woman a stranger too, although she shared my features. Or the features I'd once had.

'I' was in a series of poses from a girlie magazine, chubby arms above my head and broad pelvis tilted, acting out a teenage idea of abandon. My face, blurred from the wrong exposure and baby fat, was contorted in a way that was almost comical – it showed someone desperate to be lost in oblivion. The man, despite his intimate proximity, was almost an afterthought.

Who was he? It didn't even matter. His features were obscured and the photographs were ordered so each was succeeded by one in which their . . . *our* . . . positions became more extreme, more grotesque.

Glancing through them I wasn't so much horrified as stunned. Just as Alexander had paid me to furnish his fantasies, he must have hired someone to produce bespoke pornography. Not that simply anyone would know how to manipulate such images. Could the computer downstairs be used to do it? With the right program, I supposed – and the right investigator. For somehow an image of my younger face had been found to put on this woman's body. It was my face, although in the later shots usually it was covered by coarse wavy hair, much longer than my own hair had ever been. I guessed the face had been digitally altered, sometimes very subtly, to get the expressions just right . . . Had Alexander photographed those expressions without my knowledge? Instead of looking for a camera in the rooms we used, as he'd claimed, had he set one up himself? Even then he'd have needed to erase twenty years to return me to a self this ungainly.

Such a project would be ridiculous, surely? It would be insanely expensive and spiteful, and yet I could think of no other explanation. Why had he done it? To make my past suit him. To make me doubt my own memory, until I only remembered this – these exercises that could leave anyone who did them unconscious or worse. Then he could keep me here in the house, his thing, forever locked into his story.

My face. The look on it.

'Show them to me,' he said.

I did not move, I could not.

Bending down to the bath, Alexander delicately took the pictures out of my wet hands, a connoisseur viewing his most precious images. But as he started to glimpse through them he appeared perplexed; his eyes closed in a scowl of concentration, the equation he was forced to contemplate was impossible. These photographs – each pose in each photo – penetrated and his body slumped. He looked like he'd just absorbed a blow.

'It's you,' he said. 'You're barely recognisable, but it is you.'

It was as though he had truly never seen them before, and for a moment I thought he would cry. His reaction seemed completely, unnervingly genuine. And watching his face filled me with panic: *Just give me some sign*, I wanted to call out, *tell me what I'm meant to do, how you want me to act!* I would have followed any direction. Right then I'd have played any part so long as he didn't hurt me. All this – the letters, the photographs – must have ultimately been done so that he'd lose control. Surely that was the point. *So do it – scream!* I thought. *Just scream!*

The tap continued its dull thud: *to die, die, die.*

I was sitting now in tepid water, hunched over, trying not to shiver and waiting for the worst. Whatever it was he'd brought me here to do.

Alexander put the images back into the envelope. He opened the door, and carried them out of the room.

III

Slowly I lifted myself out of the bathwater. The air was moist and streaked the mauve walls. An old towel hung on the rail; it scratched when I used it to dry my skin, all the while listening for some sign of where in the house Alexander waited. Placing my hand on the doorknob, I half expected it to be locked. It turned smoothly and I braced, walking into the master bedroom.

The view from the window was of perfect stillness: it could have been a painted screen, a pleasing country scene of sky and endless green.

My clothes had been removed. The dress and tights and underwear I'd worn the night before had been strewn around the floor. Now they were gone. I looked over at the bed we'd lain on. It was carefully made, the quilt of lilacs pulled taut. The bedside cabinet's objects were in the right order; the commode waited for another invalid. Tightening my clasp on the towel, I put one foot in front of the other, moving fast along the frigid hallway to his sister's old bedroom.

My suitcase was missing.

Opening a drawer of the chest, I found it empty. I opened a second drawer, a third: my clothes were gone. There was now no sign I'd ever been in this room. The furniture had been straightened, the curtains tied back. It was identical to when I'd first arrived, except that on the carefully made bed he'd placed a white dress.

The sight of it winded me.

I felt I had seen it in that exact position before – this cold white thing lying lifeless, yet not entirely dead. It was not the dress from the picture of his mother. It seemed cheap, like the ones on wire hangers in opportunity shops; an unnatural white with the label wilted grey from someone else's sweat. This dress had a high sheer collar and a lace bodice trimmed with tiny plastic seed pearls. The sleeves were puffed. The sateen skirt was long and full. Even touching it to pick it up was repellent, but he'd left me nothing else to wear.

I unzipped the dress like it could hurt.

The fabric stuck to my still damp skin as I threaded myself inside, and soon I was caught in tulle and boning, caught in the dress as in a white wave. *I left home to escape, and here I am being rolled.* Through the fabric I made out weak pink sunlight – and I found myself wondering whether soldiers packed white flags before leaving for battle. Sewn into the lining of their kitbags, hidden in the way of oxygen masks on aeroplanes – did they try not to look at them while the bullets flew but feel good knowing they were there?

Downstairs Alexander would be waiting for me and I would have to do as he said, be who he required.

With the dress half on, I breathed in the scent of other brides: their joy and fear and hope and remorse. This closeness made me sick, the smell so personal. *You win. I lose. I will love, honour and obey you.* A wedding or death? I supposed the choice was simple. This dress would be my white flag. All the air leaving one's lungs just to say the words: *I do, I surrender.*

Walking down the grand staircase, I assumed Alexander would be waiting at the bottom. It was bad luck for him to see me like this before the wedding. It meant we would need to marry as soon as possible. I'd use the flowers from last night as my bouquet. When the staircase turned, I turned too, the great arched window behind me as I descended. No music and no one watching.

The entrance hall was empty. I paused, listening.

He'd lit a fire in the drawing room, and I went to it, trying to feel the flames' heat.

In my head, I began composing an explanation for my family. *By the time you read this, I will be someone's wife. I realise this seems sudden but I think you will approve.* The elastic ruffles of the dress's sleeves cut against my flesh. *My husband, Alexander, is the owner of a vast cattle property that has been in his family for five generations. I know – imagine me a farmer's wife! . . .* This was the kind of note the teenager in those photographs would write, I thought dully, full of breathless exclamation marks and little turns at bragging. *You should see my engagement ring, it's huge!* I needed instead to reassure them: *Alexander is hard-working and very traditional. In some ways, I've truly never been happier.*

If we now raced to Reverend Wendy's church and made our vows, there could still be a party in England. So sitting on the sofa,

I started to list the people I would want to invite to my wedding, then I listed the people I had to invite. The second list was long and kept growing. I preferred the idea of an intimate ceremony, but I would need to ask my extended family: my aunts and uncles, my cousins and their spouses, most of whom we'd put at tables some distance from Alexander's acquaintances. Then there were my parents' friends, whose offspring seemed to marry relentlessly, for whom it would be a snub not to send an invitation in return . . . I was listening for some sign as to where in the house he was.

Before you marry, it seems, your life flashes before you. I thought of the other designers in the office, and the students I'd known at college, and my friends at school, such as I'd had them: the secrets and the promises, and the murky, jungle-like nature of girlhood; the drawing of treasure maps and wedding dresses, and he loves me, he loves me not . . . *I am sorry if I've ever caused you worry – if anything happens to me, please remember I think the world of you.*

Alexander was standing in the doorway, expressionless. He'd put on a jacket to match the dark-grey trousers he'd been wearing, and I realised it was the suit I'd seen hanging upstairs. There was a flower in his lapel, a steel-grey silk tie loose around his neck.

I met his eye and he turned away, moving slowly towards the fireplace as if still absorbing bad news. For a long while he stared at the flames. When he spoke his voice was flat: 'Liese, you know, I hope, that I think you are an exceptional person.'

A pressure behind my breastbone.

For a moment he said nothing further, shaking his head. 'I have been thinking hard about this. You, you mean everything to me, but I can't . . . I just don't think I can go through with a wedding.' He glanced over with a look of pained innocence. 'I knew you would be disappointed.'

Suddenly I did feel something identical to disappointment, and even through my fear this infuriated me, it disgusted me. 'But why?'

'Why what?'

'Why are you calling this off?'

'Surely I don't need to explain,' he said softly. 'Still, it doesn't come easily.'

'Tell me the reason!' I heard myself shouting.

He hesitated.

'There isn't just one reason. I just do not . . . I am just not convinced that the two of us are going to bring out the best in one another, all right?' He sighed as though breathing were too much effort. 'I'd like to believe it could happen, but I don't feel convinced.'

'You think I will drag you down?'

Alexander's doleful look was confirmation. 'I didn't say that.' He sighed heavily again. 'Ending what . . . we have was always going to be hard. Oh God, Liese, please don't cry.'

With those words I started weeping – I wept to be sitting wearing a dress this white. I'd never thought I would, and probably never would again. And then I kept on weeping, after a while not entirely understanding why. Was it because, after everything I'd been through, I was at last free? Or because I was not *not* free? Was I crying at what I had suffered, or because I'd be suffering it no longer? I'd been imprisoned, tormented, and now jilted. Taking the ring from my finger, I threw it at him.

It hit the carpet and eddied under a chair.

'I can understand why you are upset,' he said calmly.

My face was collapsing. The sobs came from deep within.

At that moment, Alexander seemed to know me better than any soul on earth. What if I *was* the girl in those photographs, whom no one would ever love? What if I had met my match and realised it too late?

'It's alright, Liese, it will be alright.' Alexander stood beside me, his hand stiffly patting my shoulder. 'You are going to find someone who can appreciate you in all your . . . dimensions, who can give you the things you need.'

We stayed with me clutching him and leaning my head against his chest. When delicately he disengaged, unclasping my hands from his white dress shirt, Alexander moved to the bureau. He picked up a folder. Inside was a neat sheaf of papers: the letters. Through the exhaustion of defeat he said, 'I want you to understand I will always keep your secrets safe. I will never let your correspondence fall into the wrong hands.'

'*My* correspondence?'

'Yes.'

Wiping my eyes on the dress's sleeve, I stopped sobbing and stared at him.

'It's been you writing to me, hasn't it, Liese?'

A chill moved over my skin.

'I feel so foolish not to have realised,' he said, 'because of course they are your letters. They have to be.'

'That's a lie.'

'Oh, come on.' He nearly laughed. 'It's over. You don't have to pretend any more.'

'You're lying. You sent them to yourself!'

Frowning as though he could already view this from a great distance: 'How would I have found your photograph?'

'You told me you were going to – remember? When I didn't have one to give you.'

'But who'd actually do that? Only someone who was mad.'

He must have planned this moment all along, I thought, and now as he played it out, dropping the first sheets of paper into the flames, their corners erupted in toxic colour, and I felt disbelief. What was the point of fighting his story? These letters had been his insurance. He could play-act wanting to marry, then produce this evidence so as to never go through with it. He'd brought in his minister; he'd found a wedding dress. But it was all an elaborate performance, a grand amusement, and to satisfy what neuroses?

I would leave his house and return to the room above my uncle's garage to finish my packing. I would board a plane out of this country and spend the flight, then months, years, wondering what irresolvable thing had happened here between us, while he would go on unscathed, a seemingly eligible pillar of the community.

Alexander watched me.

'I don't really understand why you did this,' he said. 'Did you mean to arouse me or yourself?'

I wanted to hit him.

'If it was for your own pleasure then you've got some sort of problem. I mean, do you hate yourself that much?'

I knew what Alexander was doing, that he said these things

to make me lose all balance. Yet as he held the last piece of paper above the flames, I stood up from the couch and tried to grab it. Those letters had changed everything; all the strict, dull landmarks of my childhood – the circling streets, the playground, the ornamental cherry and holly and claret ash – were now alight and, in my mind's eye, would stay that way. But although I'd remember the places the letters described, and what my body was said to have done there, how would I recall what the letters said about me and who I was? This was like waking and grasping a dream's string of visions but not their cumulative meaning. I'd gone inside my head – I'd been taken right inside my head – and as I watched this last page burn I felt that some essential revelation was lost. And with it went the clue to who had won.

'Come with me.' It was all he said.

By the back door, where his father's shotgun was usually kept, my suitcase waited. While I'd been sitting in the bath he had packed my clothes, folding within them the unmarked envelope of money.

Picking up the case, he told me plainly, 'There's a train leaving Marshdale station in fifty minutes. If we move fast, you'll make it.'

He could not look me in the eye, and suddenly I was too uneasy to look into his.

'So, you're ready?'

I'd expected to at least change out of the dress. 'Just as we are?'

'Just as we are.'

I followed him into the crisp, cold light. It seemed absurd that the trees were still growing, that the sun kept powering on. The sky matched the dirty brightness of my gown, and all the colours of the garden appeared more brilliant than before. In the whiteness, buds burst from the camellia bushes as if competing for attention. A speckled bird hung from a globe of rich petals, bending the branch double. Grass shivered underneath, waiting for a fall.

Alexander opened the Mercedes door, glancing past me as I got in.

The car rolled slowly over the land: we had nothing left to say as he steered between the poplars, his knuckles pale against the wheel. We passed the markers I'd seen only three days earlier – the bone-coloured fields, the flocks of pink birds, those mountains faded blue in the direction of the sun. On the crest of the rise, I could make out the dark canopy of the national park, and the highway running in the other direction. The indicator started its second by second pulse. I leaned back to watch the road. The dashboard clock said 3:09 in electric red. Our time was up.

ACKNOWLEDGEMENTS

I wish to thank the State Library of Victoria for the support of a Creative Fellowship.

The extract on page 113 from Philip Larkin's 'The Whitsun Weddings' is from *The Collected Poems* (Faber and Faber, 1993), quoted with the permission of the publisher.